The Glowing Blossoms That Kept the Roots Alive

Amna Agib (Bit Nafisa)

TSL Publications

First published in Great Britain in 2020
By TSL Publications, Rickmansworth

Copyright © 2020 Amna Agib Mahmoud (Bit Nafisa)

ISBN / 978-1-913294-00-7

Cover image: photo by Amna Agib of vase made of Kaolin clay in 2004 by the visual Artist Suzan Adil Khanji. Suzan is an Academic, Archaeology Researcher and a PhD student. Her design consists of two leaves embracing each other. Suzan was inspired by the shapes and life of plants.

Table of Contents

.

Point of View

Judith Vonberg, Communications Officer, Migrant Voice

In *The Roots that Gave Birth to Magical Blossoms*, Amna's first book, she offers us a telescopic view into the lives and souls of her characters. It leaves the reader with the vivid impression of having encountered a series of strangers, who quickly become our friends.

Any urge to know where and when each "story" is set quickly fades as we realise these details are immaterial – each story is about this particular human being, and about being human.

The stories or reflections hit hard – there's war, death, domestic violence, abuse, bullying – but at the heart of each, there is family and there is love. They are also reflections on migration, on the natural need or desire to move around and the challenges that face us when we do.

Amna has an unusual style of writing but one that frequently steals your breath away. The strangeness, the vividness and the pinpoint accuracy of some of her descriptions are truly remarkable.

Her voice – and those of her characters – are much needed in today's world where those who cross borders are so often stigmatised. She offers a rallying cry for a different, more humane, world.

A message From Patricia Woods

I have learnt so much from Amna: her family, her life, her country of origin and her writings. It has been a privilege to be able to review Amna's books with her. The descriptive words she uses never cease to amaze me. Her grasp of current situations to encourage everyone to be empowered, whatever their situation, is humbling.

If one phrase can encourage you to open this book ... "She resembled a red-eyed candle that continuously cried" ... Open the book, enjoy, question and make a difference.

Just Reflections

I don't want to introduce myself in the traditional way of where I originally come from, how old I am, what I have studied, where I work, what my hobbies are and so on. Instead, I would like to introduce myself in a way that exposes the heart-breaking tragedies of those most in need.

Many may assume advantages are handed on a golden plate with no responsibilities. Therefore, they take them for granted with no regard to those around them.

Looking into my life, I realise how lucky I am. However, for countless people, it was not only luck that let them down.

I have achieved a high level of education, but what about the many girls denied this right?

I lived in humble homes, whereas many are sleeping rough in all sorts of weather, including that caused by climate change.

I was able to provide a decent life for my family, wondering how many of those who were orphaned by war or injustice, never experienced being part of one. They may have been adopted by gangs or dodgy dealers somewhere out there in our streets. The settings there may have been introduced as the ideal alternative. Most probably, they ended up being stabbed and bled to death before help arrived.

I lived and worked in different countries, then again, others' world, was just a tiny hut, "at nowhere". They were crammed, like sardines in a tin, waiting to be eaten by sharks.

Whilst I travelled to many places, some can't reach the only hospital in the region, on time, by foot.

Why do some people in our era still have no right to live in dignity? Why is there exclusion, marginalisation or prejudice, when we are all human beings?

As much as I tried, I couldn't wash away my pain and theirs as we were being labelled or discriminated against. We were faced with unfairness and being undermined in the process.

That is the heavy burden I have to carry on my shoulders, till freedom, peace and justice are the universal civil rights for all of us.

I am sure that day will come soon.

During my life journey, I came across several things which were different. They have challenged some of my views. What matters is that, I gained many positive experiences that strengthened my own principles as well as improved my attitude. At the very least, it helped me uncover a very tiny portion of the greed of those who deliberately cause harm to people.

I don't call myself a victim, neither should you. I believe the real ones are those who misuse their human quality. Abusing power is the foundation to instigate hatred. To complete the sequence, they use: colour, ability, religion, economic status or other characteristics as tools. They try in vain to legitimise their actions across the globe. They desperately want to feel good about themselves.

In many communities there is a saying, "divide to rule". This is exactly what they aim to achieve. I wonder how they would be able to escape the terrifying inner numbness that will haunt them forever.

If you look your intimidator in the eyes, you can somehow feel the agony of their failure. Many describe the eyes as the mirror of one's soul.

To conceal their inability to put up with the guilt, they avoid looking straight into your eyes but stab you in the back.

Some may say: that is life!! It shouldn't be.

I would like to use a bit of history, which came to mind writing these reflections. It is about Sir Isaac Newton. This English mathematician, physicist, astronomer and author, lived in the seventeenth century. Allegedly, he turned a fall of an apple from a tree into an incredible discovery, Gravity. The simplest definition for it, as I understand, is the force that attracts a body towards the centre of the earth. It keeps us upright.

His discovery coincided with the period when he was thinking about the forces of nature. My point is that, by just thinking about those who were on the peripherals, a "gravity" moment may cross our conscience and pull them to the centre of our communities. It may also keep them "alright".

Our prime responsibility, as human beings, is to preserve humanity so we can all enjoy our lives in peace.

All those who were once stung, sooner or later will produce an "antidote", equality.

I believe my book is a tiny drop in an ocean, to make things right. I hope these reflections will provide you with a hint about some of the issues I have brought up.

Introduction

I originally wrote some of these reflections in Arabic a long time ago, when I was a school girl. I didn't translate them word for word; I just captured the essence. It was shocking that some of the issues raised, remained the same to date. For some communities, it extended over the years. They might have only been refined or digitalised.

In my first book, "The Roots That Gave Birth to Magical Blossoms", all the reflections were based on distant memories passed to me by my late mother. They showed how women's experience in closed societies paved the way for their present achievements. Hence, I chose "The Glowing Blossoms That Kept the Roots Alive", as a title for this book to celebrate the many roots and generations.

All I shared, rose from within different cultures, experiences and worries. They have been transformed into applauded successes by the younger generations. My current book is a natural continuation to reinforce those achievements, which were initiated by the roots.

I tried to present the chosen topics in a way that reflects the views of both men and women of different ages.

I really benefited from the feedback I received from my valued readers. I look forward to receiving your honest views on this book, which are vital for my progress to be a better writer.

I would like to thank my dearest friend Patricia Woods for supporting me all along. I have learnt a lot from her about the real life in the UK, not to mention editing my writings. The funny part was when she tried to correct some literally translated phrases from Arabic, my mother tongue language.

To those who don't know Arabic, it is a very rich language. Its alphabet is read and written from right to left. I always argue with Pat on which word comes first. I feel, my brain automatically translates my thoughts from Arabic to any other language. It is surprising that I process what I want to say during conversations into Arabic first, then convert it into English before I speak. All this happens immediately without affecting the speed of my conversation or understanding. What a natural digital facility we have, our brain. Sometimes the sequence gets muddled especially when I am emotional.

I can't imagine in which language I really feel. What I am certain of is the fact that I was always moved by my own characters. I sometimes cry, laugh, feel outraged or optimistic, re-reading what I have written. It might seem a bit strange that I created the whole content, yet I relive their tales and experience their emotions. I also can't imagine in which language I dream. What an astonishing concept!

Each reflection I presented, signifies someone out there in our complicated universe. They might be: my country fellow citizen, an individual from a totally different community to mine or someone whom I just met wherever I travelled. Thus, the feeling I experienced towards their issues, feels the same.

Thank you, Pat, for capturing all the exceptional moments we loved, navigating our way through. I sincerely do cherish your friendship and the precious time which we had together, within the whole irreplaceable journey, including those occasions, when we felt burned out trying to perfect the book.

I specifically value the encouragement of my family and friends for their honest and sometimes tough comments.

Thank you, Professor Mahmoud Eltayeb, Dr Julie Anderson and Dr Abdelrahman Ali for your priceless help.

Thank you Karen for the amazing challenge you presented to me. It opened my eyes to a totally different concept, which I haven't considered before.

Nadir, Nazar, Muwafag, Hind and my son, Yasir, I appreciate your invaluable help.

My gratitude goes to Pinner Writers' Group. I also thank all those who supported me dearly, including you who took the time to read my books. I hope you all will enjoy it.

I would also like to highlight the good work *Migrant Voice* is doing to support those who, for whatever reason, found themselves in a totally different environment. They have to cope with whatever is thrown at them. This includes the ever-lasting scars which they obtained in their many diverged pathways.

My sincere appreciation goes to Anne Samson, my Publisher, who went beyond what is expected of her to support me, during a very difficult time. She encouraged me when I was so low. She was extremely patient with me when I was not sure of what to expect, writing my first ever book, which happened to be in English. I struggled trying to reach a balance between how I felt and what would be the impact of what I have written on my readers.

Whenever I was scared or hesitant, Anne was always there encouraging me and holding my hands. Thank you, Anne.

As a result of the support you all provided, I am publishing my second book. I hope it will make a difference. If only one person, whom my topics have represented, is helped, I will feel this book has been worthwhile.

To everyone who comes across my books, I hope I don't disappoint you.

Dedication

Taking my writing forward, my thoughts go to my late Uncle Salah Ahmed Ibrahim, peace rest upon his soul. I send this message to him, in the hope that he can feel it, wherever he is.

"It is our destiny to live scattered everywhere. We are always in a constant deliberation with ourselves to get the best out of us. Isn't the end of life but death? Yet we feel frail, scared and puzzled when it reaches our territory.

I can now sense the impact of the exile that slayed you daily. It leaves anyone, in that situation, with a hunch that they were squashed into a tiny seashell-like chunk. Drifting away by the many "feeling lonely" moments, became the norm. The hard truth is being exposed to the sour taste of not feeling the same anymore and everywhere.

Visualizing your dialogue with the "Migrating Birds", flying home in Autumn, was something else out of this world. Whilst being immersed into that poetic mystic moment, someone deliberately stole it. They pushed me into the deep end, then tapped on my shoulder telling me to take the situation as an experience. What cruelty was that?!!!

My superior, tried hard to be seen as a nice person, sent me a Christmas card. It screamed with an abusive, racial message.

Sometimes I feel helpless, thinking or convincing myself that it is me, who let it go. Is it? The naked truth is that it never dies away.

Forgive me for abandoning as much as resisting my pen for a while, even when other pens continued forward. They are now far ahead. I lost the ability to differentiate things. Scared, maybe. All the attempts returned to me disheartened and shaken. I want to believe I am not a low-spirited individual. At times, deflating feelings took over. It leaves me unable to understand why, whilst, surrounded by the crowd, I just feel lonely.

I was unable to finish the story then. A shivering of warmth towards my pen goes throughout my body now.

Was it wrong, passing a rule of its assassination then? Was it wrong trying to push it downwards even when it was ready to roll upwards?

I remember you saying, it didn't need to be the one or the other, dropping away or rising. I clearly see the vision now. Sometimes I feel like I have a broken ankle that holds me back. Could you see bewilderment jumping at me from all directions, as I just think about the coming step? It strangles my heart, which turns grey due to the lack of fresh oxygen from our Motherland.

The ability to recognise facts appears upside down. When your personal success turns against you, only grief will remain by your side. Equally, when a person loses their hope or enthusiasm, it is certain, their success would be easily displaced.

Through the dark, gloomy atmosphere, a bright spark always fills the horizon. This phenomenon was clearly represented by a familiar, gentle, unified powerful voice. The echo resonated at each corner of the globe chanting *"Tasgot Bas"*, meaning "just fall ... that is all".

The streets, roads, lanes, villages and cities were filled with hope for a better life, that we all deserve.

Surely, you recognised the voices of the magical blossoms. They are our forgotten generation. As you know, they were born and shaped by the darkness of the lifeless conscience of that era. They have not been trusted enough or we have lost faith in them all together.

Look. The roads were filled with doctors, lawyers, students, workers, young people, old people, disabled people and children holding their mothers' hands. They are demanding their rights of freedom, peace and justice. I can't see the end. Everyone was there, including the blessing of those who, put in the fundamentals for us, then said goodbye. The generation gap, the class, tribal and racial conflicts had suddenly disappeared.

Listen. The echo travelled faster, reaching out far beyond the beloved country, despite the cracks that ripped the one heart apart. It reached all the unresponsive ears of those with dead hearts, forcing them to take notice. They tried to disregard it; except they were defeated. There is no escape from the roaring voices, for those who killed the innocents. They thought they would kill a nation. They were proven wrong. What an ignorance.

The most frightening moments for the killers, were when our people lived up to their promises. They crafted a beautiful, peaceful act. Many were killed for being brave, as they refused to surrender. Others were targeted, for watching over our treasured nation or defending our human rights.

God save our Magical Blossoms that kept the soul of our roots alive. Now you can rest in peace Uncle. Our nation is in brave, honest, young and determined hands.

The Glowing Blossoms that kept the Roots Alive

*Kandaka and her husband Zac, studied in a university where they met. They were fascinated by history. Their goal was to connect the past with the present to help mould a brighter future. In addition to history they studied archaeology.

It was not a coincidence that her name was Kandaka. Her family was so proud of their ancestors' achievements. The name brought to people's memory, the Queens of the Ancient Kingdom of Kush, which had flourished, a long time ago, between 2500BC and 550AD.

In their heyday, it was extended across a territory from the Second Nile Cataract to the Junction of the two Niles at Khartoum, the capital of the now, Republic of the Sudan.

Kandaka, Zac and their families regarded people's storytelling as a powerful tool. It helped them to salute their past, revive the good experiences, learn the lived lessons and shape the relevant future. It allowed them to uphold the factual past on the face of the distorted present.

Their adventure started when they realised that both were charmed by the natural lifecycle of the plants that keep their kind alive. It inspired them to observe how the glowing blossoms keep the spirits of the roots alive.

They set off wandering in remote places, talking to people about the unwritten history of their communities. They analysed what they heard, to learn about the life of their ancestors. Many strange, brave stories were told. These stories were about warriors who protected their communities using basic, handmade weapons. They were very effective having a target-oriented function, rather than a mass destructive one. In fact, they had multiple uses. Mainly they were used for hunting. Having said that, they were also used for tackling some security issues. On top of that, they were deemed as symbolic souvenirs, which they usually exhibited at their many seasonal festivals.

Kandaka and Zac appreciated how people took a pride in their way of life, which others may have seen as primitive. They learnt how any neighbourhood, at that time, was regarded as a badge of

* The picture represents Stela with the Goddess Amesemi and Queen Amanishakheto (SNM 313380), (photo Rocco Ricci © The British Museum)

honour, no matter how it was judged by others. The styles might be so bizarre, yet they had provided pleasure to their communities.

The many exposed ruins demonstrated ancient beautiful civilisations. They held on tight to life, to tell their own history.

At the end of the couple's journey, they documented their observations, reactions as well as their interpretations of what they had seen.

Here is their account:

"At the heart of a magnificent place, darkness dominated its holy core due to an unusual backwards movement that stunned history. It reinforced the horror, division, hatred with the intent to supersede the roots.

The eye-catching green scenes of the valleys were flooded by "the forever pouring" warm blood. The destruction of the amazing, widely diverse cultivated landscape was beyond belief. It stripped the fields of its natural, soft, green lining, leaving them moaning. They were humiliated by the weight of their failure to shield themselves, as they felt exposed.

The sky closed its doors, keeping away its generous torrential rain that used to embrace the land and keep the souls alive. It provided happiness. What remained, if any, were a few thin droplets that hung between the sky and the earth. They evaporated before even touching the ground.

The migrated rivers took with them the exceptional taste of sea food. The dignity of different-sized water passages stumbled as the banks around them shrunk to disappearance level. They left behind a bleak picture, which was once a world exemplar of natural fine art.

The reservoirs turned into beggars in the streets, asking for drops of water as the sea transformed into a mirage.

The security was abandoned and the National Anthem turned into ghostly readings. The eyes dried, as tears were sold in the black market. The generously giving mothers' breasts dried up, leaving the tongues of newly born babies, hanging out in shame.

Dehydrated trees stood tall reflecting the then respected homeland. They burnt the eyes of onlookers with the reflection of the excessive heat which was stored in their broken hearts. They failed even to tremble in response to the blustery winds that crossed the deserted fields. The gales had absorbed all the hotness of the man-made Sahara in their way. They were saturated with a great rage, taking the side of the suppressed people.

The effect was felt by people, animal and places alike. They suffered from the act of those who lost their moral compass. With no prior warning, life had stopped." **The End.**

Returning home, the two archaeologists decided to put together a collection of stories, before starting history classes in their community. It was fascinating to witness how the Nubian Queens (Kandakas) had ruled a number of kingdoms many years back. So, they decided to hold women's classes first to honour those Queens. Obviously, nobody attended to start with. People have many other burning priorities, rather than learning ancient narratives. They struggle to keep their daily necessities going, besides fulfilling other obligations.

Taking into consideration the harsh reality, Kandaka and Zac, gave up their dream, until one of their friends took an interest in their project. His ambition was beyond their imagination. He had an artistic vision which helps people activate the sensible side of the brain.

A knock on the house door was heard, followed by a loud male voice.

"Good morning Gina." Gina means the Queen.

"Who is there?"

"I am Travis, the son of Aden."

"Whooo ...?"

"Travis, Grandma. Open the door."

"Mira went to the shop to bring bread."

"Grandma open the door ... I came to see you."

He waited for a long time till she found her head scarf, grabbed her walking stick, then started looking for her glasses everywhere.

"Travis, I can't find my glasses."

"You wear them around your neck Grandma."

She laughed loudly. "Found them."

Travis came in.

She offered to make tea. "Thank you, Grandma, I just had one at home.

"Grandma, remember you used to tell me bedtime stories, when I was young."

"You liked them, didn't you? ... Hahaha."

Before she started another theme, he sat beside her and continued.

"How about you telling new ones to young girls. I will read them for you first."

Her face lit up. She had a dazzling look, just like an early morning sunshine. She accepted the offer immediately.

Her mind was sharp despite her age.

That was how the classes started. In addition, they organised trips, produced documentaries and a tourism company to raise money to expand their project.

Lots of young people who heard the stories from Gina became teachers, storytellers, historians, explorers, archaeologists and tourist guides.

Years after, a huge history museum was opened. At its entrance there was a life size portrait of Gina, surrounded by those of Kandaka, Zac and Travis. On all the sides of the portrait, there were beautiful drawings of distinctive, shiny flowers. Each represented an ancient province. The modern regions were also incorporated.

Under the portraits it read, *These are four icons of the many blossoms that kept the roots alive.*

Meaning Just Fall ... that is all

To any Dictator, who thinks they could kill a nation, we say:

When Nations roar ... that is all
People want your downfall
Tasgot Bas ... is their wish
"Freedom ... justice"
is their goal
killing an innocent ... is your call

≈ ≈ ≈

A doctor's death ... is a nation's fall
Shooting one ... slaying all

≈ ≈ ≈

A teacher killed ...
A child sung ...
"Oh, my teacher ...
please forgive us
You have taught us...
(The shot will not kill ... silence does)

Oh, my teacher"
"We were out ...
To hug your hope and hold it tight
To keep it safe ... the peace is the light
No for guns ... detains and fight"

≈ ≈ ≈

We chose peace ...
Blood and torture ... on his side
Yet he dances ... laughs inside
But we know ... he always bite
Sold his soul ... killed his (zol[*])
he can't hide

≈ ≈ ≈

We would say
Tell your Dad ... tell your child
Enough was paid to kill his teacher
to kill that child

≈ ≈ ≈

Tell your Mum ...
The roads were filled
with people's voices ... day and night
Peacefully asking ... for their rights

≈ ≈ ≈

Just, you tell her ...
you went wild
It was your chance ... to win that fight

≈ ≈ ≈

---

[*] Zol is a Sudanese word used when addressing each other.

22

Just, you tell her
You had fun ... It was alright
(*Tasgot Bas*)
we all out
Bringing back the stolen rights
Civilian rules ... the unity delights
Love and peace
to stop all wars
to stop all fights
(*Tasgot Bas*) ... You have lied
Killed your zol ... You can't hide
(*Tasgot Bas*)

Alhaboob ~ The Sand-Storm Satan

Growing Up

Malak grew up in an orphanage. Visiting the place, silence and self-indulgence hits you in the face, the moment you step in. No history, no stories, no memories or hope were available to be revealed. There were even no personal files.

Malak, which means an angel, was a tiny girl with interesting, deep eyes that take you to the unknown. You feel compelled to try to explore the mystery behind them.

Malak was adopted by a middle-class traditional family. They did their ultimate best to educate, as well as raise, her to a good standard.

As planned, she graduated. Her favourite subject was psychology. In particular, she was interested in infant behaviour. She chose to work in a nursery, as if she wanted to compensate for her lost childhood.

Her adopted family set off to work in a small village at the edge of a Sub-Sahara region. The name of the village was strange and puzzling. It was known as Alhaboob ~ The Sand-Storm Satan. No one knew the reason behind that name. All they had knowledge of was the fact that the sand storm regularly revisited the region.

Alhaboob was a powerful, violent tornado. It uprooted trees as well as destroyed whatever came in its way. It also had a distinctive sound which unveiled its arrival. Following its path, vision was obscured as darkness filled the horizon. The hearts filled with fear, till it subsided.

People usually came together to pray and read "the learnt by heart" specific religious verses to release the distress. One would hear the gentle humming in the background.

Despite being so harsh, they believed, it was a blessing from God as it scattered the seeds over the fields. It also cooled the burning heat as gentle drops of rain introduced Autumn. The scenario rapidly changed. The crops boomed as a sign of a good harvest. The atmosphere became soothing: cows and goats produced rich milk, chickens provided golden eggs, local factories produced superb quality goods. It ended with trade rocketing high. That time was regarded as fertility season; hence, all marriages took place.

Above all, people believed that the whole process was a way of receiving messages from God. They were certain Alhaboob was sent by God to wipe away the sins of people who followed Satan. During that period, people reconnected with God in so many different ways: asking for mercy, conveying their gratitude, amongst others. They also sought forgiveness from neighbours, families and across the community. Several religious activities took place. They all read the entire Holy Book, shared food with those who were poor, sick or less fortunate. They also performed a special prayer to ask for a good, rainy season.

Village Life

Malak settled well in the village. She was appointed the Head Teacher in the only school for girls.

The family were given a house at the edge of the village, which was spacious and pretty. It was surrounded by a well-maintained garden, with various flowers. Malak saw many trees which she hadn't seen before. The garden was home for a wide range of birds.

Their house stood alone. It was totally different from the others. There was a narrow stream which separated it from the locals' territory.

The villagers usually lived in compact houses, which were built with mud. Their roofs were supported by tree branches. That way they suited their local warm environment, as no air conditioners were known then.

In the village there was a small clinic which was run by a para-medic. It had very basic equipment. It received essential medicines and supplies, from the Government.

Adjacent to it stood another building surrounded by a hedge. It was run by a female nurse as well as a midwife. It was a traditional healing clinic. It mainly used herbs, which were the main ingredients of ancient recipes. They were recognised for healing the most complicated cases. As documented, the ancient herbs were considered the basis for modern pharmacology.

The majority of patients were women with complicated pregnancies. There were also other patients, who were at late stages of different conditions.

There was collaboration between the two establishments. Collectively they decided who to send to the nearby hospital, which only differed, by having a doctor. They might have additional basic medical apparatus, if they were lucky. Some medicine had been stored for too long.

That hospital was about two hours' drive. One can imagine the state of the patient, who was referred, taking (maybe) their last ever journey, alive. The most heart-breaking situation was when a lorry that brought a severely malnourished, dehydrated and anaemic child, turned back with the body, even before it switched off its engine. It just broke the mother's heart into pieces, at that moment of optimism. A second before, she was full of hope, as his life was ahead of him. The wails were the only companion for the family on the return journey.

Witnessing all that, Malak decided to challenge this harsh reality in the village which she called home. Suffering was not a stranger to her.

She suggested establishing classes for women and girls in the evening, whilst husbands, brothers and sons were enjoying themselves in what they called "the club". In the club they played cards, drunk home-made juices and shared food.

The traditional menu basically consisted of: Fol (brown beans), mixed with feta cheese, tomatoes, spring onion, garlic and falafel. It was essential to use different exotic spices. Above all, it was necessary to add red and green fiery, taste-bud offending chillies. The recipe would not be complete without a flood of sesame oil over the surface as the king's crown. This was equivalent to "the icing on the cake".

The men would wash their hands before sitting in groups around big trays. Ahead of attacking the meal, it was a must to loudly say; "In the name of God, the merciful and gracious". They would eat with their natural cutlery, their right hands.

During these daily gatherings, all the village affairs would be discussed. Very important decisions were taken around the (Fol) dish.

Women had their own gatherings as well, but no village affairs were included. Instead they shared beauty secrets and female matters only.

Malak's initiative for adult education was eventually rejected, as expected. Later, her father used his influence to convince the men to support his daughter. In return, he donated a huge sum of money, by the standards of the village, to renovate and upgrade the club. Men followed suit, contributing as much as they could afford. Shortly after, following that day, the project was established. The village embraced a change that put it in the right direction.

Malak spoke with the most regarded and respected senior women, who played an unofficial council's role. They had a great, unlimited power with huge influence within the women's community.

Reluctantly, they supported the idea. The reason behind their approval was to limit the threat to their power posed by Malak. They put a red line for her, which she shouldn't cross. The council only permitted her to teach cookery lessons. As a gesture of goodwill, they suggested to Malak, to add sewing, if she wanted to.

It was apparent to Malak that this group of women were scared of losing their status to the younger generation. The girls were obviously quick learners, as they could easily grasp the basics of modern education and technology.

Malak agreed the condition knowing that winning them over would be the most desirable cornerstone for her to take the first step on the success ladder.

The suggestions were generally welcomed by almost all the women and girls. Before the first meeting to launch the project, Malak deliberately reached out to those who lived in the shadow. They were not expected to attend general meetings. Surprisingly, they came with breath-taking ideas, backed by very convincing arguments. She agreed not to mention their names, as they requested. Precisely, that was what happened in the school yard when the first meeting was held. During that evening almost all residents attended, including the men. That way, Malak won all sides as she introduced the idea.

The senior women endorsed the proposals, which were agreed at the meeting. In a clever, well thought-out act, they volunteered to follow up the actions. The idea was to control the project and to introduce it in their own way. That was their approach to secure the continuity of their power. Malak ignored the hidden agenda and showed her gratitude for their kind cooperation.

That way, she left everyone happy believing they had won the race. She gained the trust of all women, girls, men and boys of all ages.

The classes were diversified to include: writing, reading, maths, first aid, maternity, childhood issues, nutrition and creative activities.

Later, many attendees graduated as: nurses, midwives, social workers and nursery teachers, amongst others.

Surely, the project had changed the face of the village for the best. A number of adjacent villages enrolled in these classes. In-no-time, the same ideas, were replicated in every part of the region.

Malak introduced another interesting initiative, "Alsandoog", which literally means the box. It was a scheme, where each member contributed an agreed amount of money. It was five local pounds, which was assumed as affordable, by many.

The most in need woman would take the first collection. This arrangement would carry on, in the same way, each month till all participants had received their sum.

They mainly, used the money to help with the costs of unforeseen crises: a speedy marriage, prematurely welcoming a new baby or an unexpected maintenance for their homes.

The idea travelled fast to reach the men's club. They created their own Sandoog, which may have had higher investments.

Following that amazing success, Malak introduced a third idea which essentially resonated with young girls. As Malak was easily able to travel around, she bought different items for sale, by interest-free instalments. She used her own money to set up the business, starting with buying clothes first. Then gradually, she introduced: jewellery, kitchen wares, in addition to other items, that were requested by a few members. Sometimes, she took individual requests to help those in greater need.

Surprisingly, she included spare parts for lorry drivers, bits and pieces for the clinic, books for students amongst others.

As the project was expanded, a number of girls were chosen to accompany Malak to help meet the increasing demands. Wealthy members sent money.

A shop owner agreed with Malak to manage the business by employing local people to run it. In return, he received a reasonable profit, which helped him support his family.

Later they discussed how to sustain their projects. Ideas kept coming, even from beyond the village.

A management committee was appointed to oversee the business. A woman was appointed as the Chair. A number of places were filled by younger, older and disabled people.

The committee was tasked with setting the budget alongside overseeing the quality of the goods. Meeting the demands was the top of the agenda. The committee was also asked to develop a sustainability plan.

That was the first time when women felt appreciated. Therefore, requests from women flooded the committee for approval: opening cafes, child-minding services, sewing shops, with new ideas, such as socialising clubs.

Construction fast emerged as a trend amongst the young. Buildings with varied designs dominated. Requests for colourful buildings rocketed high. Previously, the village used to have houses with the colour of natural mud only.

Their work continued many years after the departure of Malak's family.

With all those achievements, Malak lived a fulfilling life, apart from a dark sided worry that led to an unexpected disappearance of the family.

This mysterious departure, with even no leaving do, left many unanswered questions amongst the villagers. Similarly, it left a cloud of sadness all over the place.

The Relived Life

During the time the family spent in the village, something unusual bothered Malak. Since the first night, she always felt a strange connection to their house. She assumed they had lived in this house before. However, she dismissed the idea straight away, as her parents had never said such a thing. Unfortunately, that thought always stayed inside her head.

Malak spent many sleepless nights imagining their rooms with different layouts. These illusions remained her daily companion. Sometimes she ignored them, but most of the time, they occupied a big part of her thoughts.

Whenever Malak struggled, she took an extreme view that people live more than one life without realising it. Her inner logical way of thinking immediately rejected that idea. "How could this be possible?"

Whenever, she had no other options, she chose to lean towards what she had strongly rejected, the reliving option. Despite the fact this validation was hard to digest, she just did in the circumstances. She would change the subject to something pleasant or take a stroll along the stream outside.

The following strange scenarios were repeated almost every morning when Malak entered the bathroom to have a shower.

At the precise moment, when the door was closed, a red basket full of baby clothes would appear in the corner. At the very top of that pile, there was always a pink lovely, shiny cover, which she adored. A similar action also took place on the opposite wall. A shelf full of baby's toiletries, was displayed. Every time she tried to reach out to it, the shelf would move away and just disappear.

She always felt shaky. To get herself back in shape, she would escape to the garden. Every time she went out, there was a sheep, a cow, a dog, with a lot of chickens running around. Some days she might notice a gardener, whom she hadn't seen before. He never looked at her. Moreover, when she attempted to speak to him, he always vanished without a trace. It seemed to her so strange.

Beyond the morning time, she didn't remember or think about the situation.

Taking all that into consideration, she was always worried coming back home after work. She told no one of this experience.

One day, she accidentally heard a woman talking to her friends, "I swear to God, every day on my way home after work, I saw a ghost in front of the ruin. It always ran away when it saw me," the woman said. "Didn't you hear the barking of the dogs at the same time, midnight?" she continued.

Before the women reacted, Malak appeared from a side road at a short distance from where they stood. They swiftly walked away, not even responding to her greeting.

Malak was extremely shocked when she heard this conversation. "I didn't even notice there was a ruin on the other side of the village. I never saw anyone going towards that direction. For me, dogs usually barked all night."

Hearing that revelation gave Malak some relief, as she assumed, she knew the truth. "I guess what I experience every morning, was performed by one of its friends."

Nevertheless, she needed some time to absorb what had just happened. She headed back home straight away, abandoning her walk about. She needed to calm herself before verifying the truth.

The next morning, she saw nothing in the corner or on the opposite wall. She ran to the garden, all the chickens, the dog and the gardener had disappeared.

Suddenly, she felt unsteady. Her head was spinning with great speed and her eyes were cloudy. Although she leant on the wall, which surrounded the house, she fell down.

She took a deep breath, lifted herself up and continued inside. She went straight to her room before her parents noticed her entrance. They thought she had been for a walk.

A couple of days later, Malak felt confident and had enough courage to head towards the deserted building. She was exceptionally nervous.

When she stepped outside their home, to visit the ruin, an unexpected fear grew inside her. It was far more intense than what she usually had, returning home at the end of each day. It was even incomparable to the bout of fear, she went through, when she entered the bathroom, to discover the disappearance of her daily scenario.

The Magical Yet Horrific Visit

At the ruin, that day, Malak heard loud men's voices, happily laughing. In the background, there was a rhythmic echo resembling a movement of heavy machinery. There was also a noise of slowly moving trucks, which were regularly beeping their horns, as they came, from far away.

She imagined seeing a familiar face, which faded so fast. She was unable to identify the features as it disappeared inside.

Although the situation was expected to be frightening for her, Malak experienced a strange peaceful, tranquil wave of heat, running through her heart. It encompassed her body. Her breathing slowed down. She was relaxed.

For a brief moment she felt as if a strong pair of hands cuddled her from behind. She expected to see her father and wondered how he guessed she was here. Her body weight felt so light. She smiled, then turned her face swiftly to no avail.

Her eyes flickered with no prospect of coming to its normal state. In a fraction of a second the place became hazy, whilst the silence disrupted her ears. Sadly, she lost the lively sounds. Everything but the darkness had disappeared. The building became cold, as it lost its vibration. She didn't feel scared. She became very upset that the situation was beyond her grasp.

With a robotic movement, she headed home.

Mum noticed her daughter looked pale. She was so distant. "What is the matter love?" No words came out of Malak's mouth, as if she had lost the ability to talk. She only mentioned the word "ghost".

Her mother hugged her to create a sense of feeling safe. She checked the temperature, which was normal. Her breathing also seemed regular. What scared her was that her daughter's eyes were widely opened. She took a long look at them. They hardly blinked. Malak threw unconnected words. In addition to the mother's horror, Malak carried out bizarre movements, up, down, forward, backwards, drawing strange circles in the air, suddenly, looking behind.

The parents were worried she might have caught an infection, witnessing her hallucinating. Knowing the capacity of the clinics as well as the distance to the nearby hospital, they decided to set off to a bigger city. It would take them three hours to reach the hospital, driving on uneven roads.

To make the picture bleaker, the roads were dark with no signs, direction or a navigator. So, the journey would only depend on the father's sense of direction.

Malak gradually started to relax, though sluggishly recovering. From the moment they left the village, until then, she said no word. She just had a sip of water during the whole journey. The status of her eyes remained the same.

In the hospital she said nothing. From what her mother described, the doctors guessed she had experienced a panic attack. They prescribed her medicine. She slept well till the morning. Luckily enough, it was the school holiday.

Malak's father made a few calls from the hospital phone, then the family continued the journey to their hometown with no luggage.

Fortunately, a visiting psychology professor was in town. He was tasked with reviewing a number of medical facilities by an international organisation. The aim was to improve healthcare in general and mental health, in particular.

The Discovery

The professor agreed to see Malak despite the fact that there were no records of her childhood to guide him. He was interested in her case, especially, as she had studied psychology with reference to children's behaviour. He admired her hard work and wondered how she had achieved such a huge success despite her young age.

To try to get to the bottom of the panic attack, together with his team, he visited the village. They spoke to locals with no specific reference to Malak. He was told a lot of interesting things, including the fact that the Head Teacher had not been seen since the school holiday. They added that it was not unusual for the family to return to their home town during the holiday. This time it was different as no one knew that they had travelled. That was why they mentioned it.

By chance, the professor's team came across the ruin. They found nothing extraordinary when they visited the ruin. There was no sign of any activity that had taken place, in decades. The professor could not hide his disappointment, as no one talked about the ruin, as if it was not there. They decided to revisit the place again at midnight.

Life was totally shut down at night. It was so dark. In the village there were no street lights to make their journey easier, finding their way to the ruin. It was deadly silent apart from dogs' barking.

When they became closer to the rundown building, the team used night equipment which was sensitive to any activity. Suddenly, it recorded a movement. The atmosphere became edgy, as they didn't know what to expect.

Generally speaking, no one confessed they believed in ghosts. The rapid rise in their breathing reflected their unconscious reaction to the situation. It was the anticipation of what they might face. Their advanced equipment soon revealed a mysterious shadow. It was just a homeless man. The team found their way in through the wreckage. A frightened man had made the ruins his home.

After offering him a good sum of money, he told his story.

"I am not from this village. I have no family. Locals don't dare to come near this building, that was why I chose it as my new home.

"Every night I go out late to collect any leftover food. It seems I compete with the stray dogs for a midnight meal for survival." He paused for some time, uninterrupted, then continued, "My father used to work here many years ago, when I was just a kid. Sometimes he took me to the factory, (the ruin).

"I remember how it buzzed with movement. The sound of the machinery always overrode that of the trucks. The workers from around the region were laughing and forming a long queue on pay day. They clapped and performed funny dances, whenever the man at the top of the line, received his payment." He took a deep breath. His eyes blinked.

"I loved that day as father took me to a nearby place. We walked around just like wandering over the moon. Our journey regularly ended at the market where my dad would buy me nice things."

At that moment he closed his eyes. A tear quietly escaped to hug his anxious face. "That is all I can remember."

He abruptly stopped. It needed some persuasion for him to continue.

Hesitantly, he went on, "My mother told me the owner of the factory, where Dad used to work, was a bad man. Workers didn't like him. He lived with his family. He had a baby girl. They lived in what looked like a palace to us, far away from the village. It was green with high walls, that prevented anybody from seeing inside.

"She also said, no one saw his family. Even when they were travelling in his big car, it was not possible to see them. The glass of the windows was dark.

"The bad guy dismissed a lot of workers, including my father, for no reason. He didn't even alert them beforehand. At least they then would have been prepared for what could happen to their families. We haven't seen my father since.

"My mum was very sad. She was extremely ill. She deteriorated so fast. Shortly after, my mother died, leaving me alone." He took some time saying nothing. The professor didn't disturb him.

"I came here to look for Dad. He would be old by now. I assume he might need my help. My mother told me to look for him. Those were her last words, before she died. She asked me to tell him that he was forgiven. I am afraid the prospect of not finding my father, is killing me, exactly as it did to my mum."

The unknown homeless man looked very sad. They offered him some juice with a piece of cake. After he had a rest, the man continued, "I remembered. Mother also mentioned that people were talking about the fate of the cruel man, "the owner of our lives" as they called him. It seemed he had disappeared after an unusually strong storm that continued for many hours." His voice became tense, "Most probably God was angered by his many sins." He appeared as if he was squeezing his mind. "I swear on my life, this is all I can remember."

The professor felt there was more to it. He tapped on his shoulder to encourage him to talk. Suddenly, the man knelt down, passionately placed his forehead on the ground for some time, as if he was praying.

"God forgive me."

The professor encouraged him, "We are also looking for the truth, just like you. You didn't give up looking for your father, did you?"

He pulled himself up. "This might just be gossip. Even my mother was not sure." No one said a word. Then he continued, "I do this for my father.

"Okay, people were talking about a little girl, who was found far from the village by a shepherd. Her tiny body was hidden under a large piece of plastic. She was encircled with a belt. She tightly held a pink cloth in her hand. Broken glass was scattered around her. She was in an appalling state. Her face was unrecognisable. She was covered in blood.

"A few workers also disappeared the same day. No one heard about the girl or the missing workers again.

"People stopped talking about the factory, my mother said. They believed it was haunted by the spirits of the dead. She also told me the name of the village was 'Alhaboob'.

"To my great surprise, when I arrived here, I found its name was changed to Alhaboob – the Sand-Storm Satan."

The professor asked the man how locals survive storms. With no hesitation he replied, "Without a doubt, the storm was always very harsh. Alhaboob was the most feared beast. It destroyed homes, uprooted the strongest trees, as well as killed livestock. God willing, locals co-existed with it. They knew its timing. It had certain signs of its imminent arrival, so they took precautions and prayed for forgiveness. That was all they could do." His eyes filled with tears and fear, except he managed to hide his face with his hands.

The team learnt that, following the incident many years ago, different versions of the same story were told. One stated that a horrendous storm with flying flames brought down the factory to the ground. Remarkably, they all agreed that the only area which was not affected was where workers received their salaries. Then, bit by bit, all the stories were rapidly forgotten. No one talked about, or entered, the destroyed factory after the tragedy.

The Professor was stunned by what he had heard. He learned a lot in his first visit. He couldn't understand how such a story was wiped from people's memories so fast. He retrieved that assumption immediately, "Maybe they deliberately did so."

The professor was convinced that Malak was that little girl who had been rescued by the shepherd. The hardest challenge for him was how to break the news to Malak and her family about her birth father. He once owned the factory (the ruin) and then disappeared following a sandstorm, together with his family.

Following the incredible revelation, the family chose not to return to the village. Locals were puzzled by their unexpected departure.

As life went on, daily challenges dominated. The family was soon forgotten, or as the professor predicted, they chose to do so.

Malak's New Life Chapter

Accepting the reality was hard for Malak to absorb. The trauma led to her total meltdown. She spent a year in mental health institutions, supported by her family.

Despite this awful life changing incident, it was a miracle that Malak picked herself up. She made a full recovery. She joined a local university to study the harsh environmental phenomena. She chose "The impact of sub-Saharan storms on communities" as a topic for her dissertation.

On the day of her graduation, Malak had the surprise of her life. When her name was called and she stepped onto the stage, the hall's doors widely opened. A massive stream of people of different ages wearing the same school uniform entered. The uniform was distinctive. It had a logo of a small box printed on the left side of the jumpers. Later, she was told the box represented her project Alsandoog. It was put on the left side to symbolize how she had occupied everyone's heart.

At the beginning, Malak didn't comprehend what was going on till they held up a placard that read, "Malak School of Alhaboob Village") Each member of the audience was holding a small box with her name printed on the top.

The first thing that caught Malak's eyes, was that "The Sand-Storm Satan" was dropped from the village name.

For a while, she stood like a frozen princess who was waiting for her prince to kiss her, to bring her back to life.

Seeing many familiar, happy faces of women, men, girls and boys of all ages filling the room, brought back memories of the good days, which she believed were erased forever. On the contrary, she felt the logo was sealed into her heart and soul.

Her eyes were watery, reminding her of the stream she loved which never stood between her and the people. She always felt she belonged to them, exactly as to it.

One of the powerful women together with the shop owner, presented her with a golden "Sandoog" with her name on the top. Opening it she saw a five-pound note, reminding her of how the village project started. Her smile widened as the surprises kept coming.

A nurse, who was her student, delivered a very sincere speech. She took the audience through the unusual journey of the village which won it an award, for changing the lives of the community. She also described how it developed to become an ideal example for the rest of the region.

Two young children entered the stage holding an award. They presented it to Malak on behalf of the entire village. She held the mic to thank them thinking that was all, but she lost her voice and was taken aback by the professor's entrance. He was accompanied by a man she hadn't met before. The man's face seemed familiar, yet she had no recollection of him. The professor introduced him first as the unknown hero, then as his co-worker who helped him to navigate the region.

"With his help, we learned about people's life stories, which they and us cherish dearly," said the professor.

The unknown hero told his life story and his connection to the "Alhaboob village". He was the same homeless man, whom the professor found in the ruin when they visited the village the first time. His story which described the factory brought back to Malak the memories of her first visit to the ruin.

Only then, she realised why his face looked familiar to her. He was from her past, a child of an employee who worked for her father, who owned the factory (the ruin). Most probably, she met him as a child, when his father brought him to the factory, the same as did her father. She looked at him with excitement. He did the same. Since then, they became friends.

He told the audience that the professor advocated, on behalf of the region, to seek support to improve people's health and well-being. As a result of his effort their village, as well as his, were selected to participate in an international project for community development.

He paused for a few moments, looked straight into Malak's eyes then hesitantly, he said, "The ruin of the factory would be demolished." He took a deep breath before he continued, "It will be rebuilt into a modern hospital equipped with all the fundamentals. Locals will be employed to run the hospital. A quota of students will be helped to study medicine to join the workforce."

He left the best for last. He continued, "A business college will be built. Guess what?" He paused. The room was quiet. "Malak Business College, I say." The silence quickly erupted into applause, roar, cheering ... just everything possible.

He continued, "It will recruit those who are able and interested in studying business, from the region."

The professor stepped to the podium, before announcing, "A special gift for a special person." He looked at Malak. With a lovely smile he said, "We will also provide scholarships to support projects that study the impact of Alhaboob on communities. We are keen to create opportunities for the new generation by equipping them with the required technology. It is their time to examine existing knowledge. They are the ones to work out new solutions for the future."

At that moment, the hall was shaken by the strength of hands put together in appreciation of the enormous volume of achievements.

They were overwhelmed how all that came out of a young, talented woman who was their "School Head".

The professor, who was representing an international organisation for community development, concluded the celebration by a question to Malak. He got down on one knee in front of her. There was complete silence. You could hear a pin drop in a huge haystack.

"Malak. Would you do me and your community the honour to be the chief executive for this huge project?"

The atmosphere was ecstatic. Everybody was laughing. A mixture of emotions erupted revealing anticipation. The professor stood up. He shook hands with Malak. Her eyes were extensively open as her heart. For a moment, Malak assumed the whole setting was a side effect of her medication. "This could have happened ages ago. It was scary then. But not now. Everything is real."

At that moment Malak felt so proud of her parents, the community, the professor, the unknown hero, not to mention, of course, herself. She held her head high, took a deep breath and laid her hand over her heart. All attendees rose up.

Malak gently whispered, "I do."

The hall was filled with joy, cheers, applause and love.

All gave her a standing ovation. People climbed the stage hugging each other. The luckiest were able to hold Malak tight for the longest possible time of two seconds.

Within three weeks the family headed back to where they belonged. The village had changed. At its heart, a very pretty house stood tall, with no stream to separate it from the beloved big family. Her adopted father's name hung on the door.

A message for the Reader – Countless years after, the traditional herbal remedies were "chemicalised and tabletised". The "Sandoog" was replaced by high interest banks. On the contrary, numerous high-value foodbanks were created to fill the gaps.

People were shocked, at how faster than homelessness, a lot of high street shops that sell sleeping bags went into administration.

Sit Al Shai ~ The Tea Seller

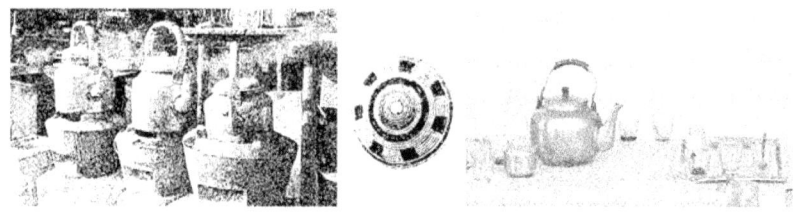

Kaltoom was an illiterate woman with a brain of a business man. There was no such thing as a business woman. Women were not entitled to that privilege where this story took place. Apparently, they were deemed powerless. In reality, they were the household powers. They managed all their family affairs, including financial matters. They would also solve all kinds of problems, to make ends meet when the bread bearer stumbled. Their skills equated to, if not exceeded, those of the businessmen.

Kaltoom graduated from the top university, the university of life. Charlie, her husband, was a low skilled self-employed worker. His income could not secure an adequate life for his many children and his elderly parents. In addition, he had a responsibility to support his parents-in-law. This was how the extended families operated.

Their children were no different to those who lived in the semi-ruined, congested neighbourhood. Their houses were casually built, with no planning permission, which was unheard of there. The household was powered by "Ratina", a special glass/metal lamp that used gasoline.

This neighbourhood was separated from a very wealthy compound by a high impenetrable hedge. Many super rich families lived behind that barrier. They enjoyed an up-to-the-minute luxurious life: Wi-Fi, private swimming pools and saunas, as everyday life's necessities.

Kaltoom's precious hope was to be able to send their male children to school, dreaming that one day they would be able to cross the impossible boundary, the hedge. In her mind, their children would be offered gate-keeping, car washing, gardening or cleaning jobs, if they took a few moves across the border.

For Charlie, that was a step too far, not a matter for discussion. In his mind, that was a fantasy or unrealistic dream which filled Kaltoom's underdeveloped brain.

Kaltoom exploited all her tactics and tricks to influence Charlie, knowing that she would win in the end. She knew how to navigate her way through her husband's rigid mind-set.

She explored with other women how they could support their families. Predictably, she won their trust, presenting to them a well-considered economic plan. One with many risks, which were worth taking. She decided to start a very convenient enterprise, selling tea on the edge of their street. She developed a social hub, where people could socialise, share stories or just feel they belong to something. Such activities were the sort of affairs that appeal to a wider sector of the society. In the area there were no other options which everyone could afford.

Kaltoom convinced the owner of the local furniture workshop to lend her a few chairs and tables. In exchange, she would provide him with a jug of tea twice a day for his workers, till the debt was cleared.

She also secured a similar deal with a small shop on the side of a narrow road. It sold cups, teapots, spoons and other essential items, which she needed to start her business.

Last but not least, Kaltoom negotiated with the grocery owner to become her supplier. In return she offered him a percentage of the profit. She also agreed to give him a discount, whenever he needed refreshments.

She was confident he would appreciate such an arrangement, which could improve his marketing strategy. People of status, like

Traffic Police Officers or his suppliers visited his humble shop from time to time. He was obliged to offer hospitality to them, in accordance with their traditions. So, the agreement seemed attractive. Without hesitation, he signed the contract with Kaltoom.

She also spoke to the local Area Administrator to avoid the unexpected tax collectors. People's total proceeds had never covered the basics, not to mention any unexpected eventuality, such as health care and what the future may hold. However, people also believed that half the collected tax would lose its way before it reached its destination.

Another thing to remember was the fact that many people in the already congested area had a considerable number of children. They also had an unwritten collective duty towards the eldest in their community, who lacked any support from the authorities.

In her circumstances, Kaltoom established a good basis that led to some jealousy from Charlie.

On the one hand, she managed to face his unexpected episodes of rage with calmness and wisdom, seeing the light at the end of the tunnel. On the other hand, he learnt to deal with all sorts of people in the street, protecting his wife.

Kaltoom became a respected member of the community. The status she owned was because of her determination. She just witnessed people's pain, desperation and loss of self-worth.

She brought together the experience of different generations around a teapot. Her project became the beating heart in a corner of a hardly known street, where people from all walks of life grew stronger together.

She always kept the place extremely clean and tidy. That way, it appealed to a wide range of people, many of whom were from other areas.

Kaltoom used sandalwood mixed with other scents to send away annoying guests; the flies which didn't mind sharing doughnuts. They quickly became addicted to the smell of mint. Of all these, it was the aroma of fresh coffee beans, sizzling on the coal fire, that had invited them. They couldn't resist it, even if they tried.

From time to time, unwanted people with huge power, disturbed the hub. Their intention was to grab a slice of everyone's tiny profit, which was cemented with peoples' sweat and worries, as they used to say. This expression was usually used by residents to convey the level of the hardship which they faced, supporting their families.

Kaltoom's business was often dragged back, as those greedy people used their power to confiscate her basic equipment. They would seize all her profit for the day, accusing her of harbouring illegal drugs, selling forbidden alcohol, if not promoting prostitution. All these crimes were regarded as extremely offensive in that community. Any of these accusations could have easily destroyed her business, her family reputation, if not the life of the entire family. Above all, the least this would have led to, was a massive fine, as officials consistently misused the legal processes.

Despite the fact that she was repeatedly targeted and sent to prison, Kaltoom would be released without a charge. The reason was the fact that, the whole community stood behind her. Every time she was detained they accompanied her to the authority's office. There were also community lawyers, who continuously volunteered to defend her. The officials did not like the presence of many people in front of their offices. They feared it would bring unnecessary attention. That was the tactic the community preferred to use. It always paid off.

As the hub advanced and grew bigger, Kaltoom thought of putting in a system to defy those selfish, mean people. If it was up to her, she would have used an ancient way, the dove messengers, to alert her. However, the rapid development of mobile phones, provided a more valid alternative.

The young customers together with the community supporters, created their own warning system. Their service covered the whole working day. They set up short rotas, which allowed many individuals to contribute to the collective effort, to keep the hub alive and Kaltoom safe.

Their system puzzled those who dreamed of catching her red-handed. Each and every time they arrived, they would only find a trace of burned coal that led them to a dead end. They left with a great disappointment. They wished for better luck next time, which never happened.

The hub had prevented many girls from falling into the wrong side of life. They employed them or helped them find work, with the assistance of their fast-growing networks. They also agreed with the local schools to sponsor some of the girls whose families were unable to meet the cost of schooling.

The hard work with women had paid off as they established an adult education centre with a nursery attached to it.

The hub had even financially supported those who were able to run small businesses. They were lent start-up loans. After their businesses flourished, they returned the original amount of the loan, which would be reinvested into new businesses.

The hub had many young helpers who were able to cross the road challenging the forbidden hedge. Luckily, it was not in the capacity of gate-keepers, carwash workers, gardeners or cleaners, as Kaltoom had fancied at that time. They did far better than that. They pursued careers in management and finance amongst others.

Charlie struggled for many years to accept the success of his wife. He secretly admired her abilities. "Above all, she supported the family, managed to extend her support to the community around us, as well as achieved far more than what was expected of her." He only said that to himself.

With a hefty foot-dragging mood, he just allowed himself to occasionally appreciate her. He might have been the latest of all to do so. Never mind, in the end he won the race against customs, traditions, pride, fear and assumptions, that had held him back for a long time.

He became her right-hand man, who was less of a "moaner for nothing" as she used to call him. Yet, sometimes he missed his old habit, muttering. Deep down he felt proud of his family. He even sought advice from his wife whom he called "Malka", which translates into Queen. With time, they all called her the same. None of them remembered Kaltoom anymore.

A few years after, the community created a local festival where a lot of tea was served. A "Queen of Tea" was selected. She was presented with a cup, teapot and a bag of charcoal. Soon, it was turned into a national day, where many activities took place. They involved school children, businesses and different communities.

To appreciate Malka's achievements, a local traditional tourist hub was built. A replica of Kaltoom's street corner was set up in the heart of the building. The original furniture and tea sets were displayed. A modern café was also built in.

They injected modern technology and used contemporary designs to increase the business productivity. For example, to highlight the experience of Kaltoom's hub, they created a video with a tune on the background. It was sung with a modern rhythm, *Sit Al Shai ... Wal Shai Ba Jai* which translated into *The tea seller and the tea were here*, inviting visitors to try a sample of the tea. It became a very valued melody. It made people feel proud of their uprising against all kinds of conspiracy to silence or suppress people. The melody was about a lay woman who fought for her family's existence.

The traditional part was more popular amongst the younger generation and the tourists than the modern part of the café.

Those who created the alert system for Kaltoom's hub were now professionals. They installed a safety system to deter troublemakers.

Many volunteers and trainees who worked in the café, gained very valuable experiences.

A big company offered to buy the place, but the offer was turned down to preserve the community spirit. The hub was protected by the National Buildings Association.

Many other traditional tea hubs were created by several communities across the country in solidarity with people's willpower to confront the odds and win their freedom.

The experience of one woman had changed the face of many neighbourhoods. Similarly, many Kaltooms and Malkas were born and shone, across the country. They exhibited a sharp intelligence that exceeded the expectation of most of the businessmen.

A Midnight Scream

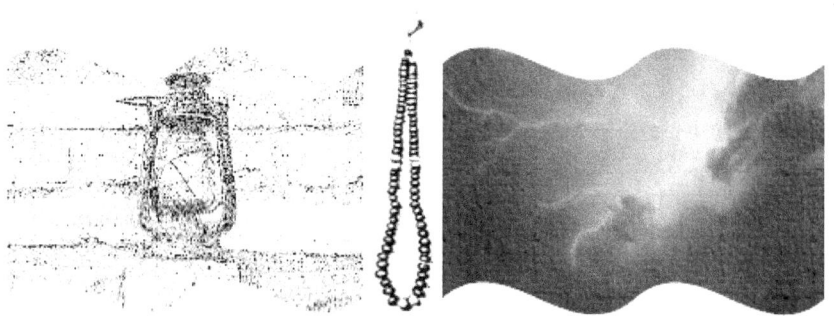

She resembled a red-eyed candle that continuously cried. The warm dripping tears hugged the fresh-looking cheeks. Sakina rested at a far corner of a tired room that suffered from a natural consequence. The landlord had failed to renew his vows to keep it well-balanced. Its wall paint was so faded which constantly reminded them of death.

Sakina stared aimlessly. Suddenly, the holy stillness of the room was broken by unclear mumbles and prayers to God for help. From time to time the calm of the room was ripped by a loud scream. It seemed to any listener as if it was the end, when in fact it was only the beginning.

Beside the old bed sat Batool, the mother, praying for the tiny tired body of her daughter to keep going. On the opposite side sat a woman with a very respectful appearance with an authoritative face. At her feet there was a small leather suitcase which contained elementary medical instruments. She had a donkey grazing outside, which assisted her travelling many miles to help women who lived faraway. They never saw a doctor or had a scan when they were pregnant.

Near the closed door, on the outer side of the room, sat a middle-aged strong man who was also reading religious verses. In his hand he held special pretty, shiny Islamic Beads (*Sibha*). It allowed him to reaffirm God's ninety-nine names to be able to accept his will. His eyes were literally hanging on the door's handle.

Everybody in the room heard the sound of the aggressive bangs of the dark clouds outside, attacking each other. They could see the bright lights, which resulted from the interaction, mixing with the heavy waterfall of the sky. It was amazing how the outside scene added its voice to what was happening inside.

Life started when a tiny indistinct head found a way out. It suddenly halted, as if it wanted to inspect where it was heading. The head was followed by a tiny greasy body, which was hanging by a cord. It gave the impression of keeping all the options open. It reserved the right to reverse the journey, and climb back, if it didn't like what it glimpsed in that second. Whilst it was still making up its mind, the respectful woman cut off its return ticket, the cord. She gave it a gentle tap on the back forcing it to cry because it started the unknown journey, with no turning back.

While this dilemma was sorting itself, the fragile mother smiled for the first time. With a hesitant, weak voice, she asked "boy or girl?"

For the disappointment of everyone in attendance, it was a girl. They felt the sticky situation that the mother found herself in. What Sakina actually wanted, was the opposite of what her husband and the community around her wished for. Without a doubt they wanted a boy who, as believed, is more useful. He can support the family, in contrast to a girl who relies on the father for life, unless she moves to the husband's dwelling and sets her father free.

The situation seemed as if it unconsciously masked the happiness. Sakina appeared miles away, and a shadow of sadness filled the tired room. She threw a wry smile staring at nothing. Her eyes were watery when she first glanced at the baby.

Barely heard, she said, "Thank God she is healthy." Then slowly closed her eyes before falling into a deep sleep.

The hands of Noor, the midwife, trembled when she held the new-born for the first time. With disappointing robotic movements, she started to clean her. It was so hard for Noor to detach herself from what was going on.

Understandably, she sympathised with the women she served, having held their hands, looked after them in their highs and lows for nine months. Any midwife in her situation would be part of every woman's story. She was trusted with their secrets, lives and that of their babies. As commonly said, "homes have secrets", the midwife was the keeper.

Batool, the grandmother, avoided looking in her daughter's eyes as she was unable to hide the bitterness, she endured. Suddenly, she remembered her son-in-law, who was impatiently waiting behind the closed door. With heavy steps which moved backwards, she opened the hefty door. It screamed, alerting the waiting man. The cold coupled with Batool's featureless face, said it all.

"Thank God they are both safe." She called him the father of the girls. The words muddled with a sound from outside adding more darkness to the drama inside. His *Sibha* fell to the ground. Strangely enough, he didn't bother to pick it up, neither did he look back. It seemed to him as if it lost all the shine it had before. Talking to himself, all the words came at once, "Why me? What have I done wrong to deserve this? I have four girls now. Who is going to look after them if I die? Life is becoming so hard along with the fact that I am not becoming any younger. I have no boy to keep my name going. What am I going to do?"

He dragged his feet and disappeared into the darkness of his room. His last words were, "God forgive me for the attempted deliberation with myself about your will."

Suad, the new-born, inherited the controversy that was associated with her birth. It is said that babies feel the tensions around them, as early as being in their mother's womb. Certainly, she felt it before and after her arrival. In addition, she also felt that angry reaction which added its voice from outside the room the moment she was born.

The world at that time was full of strange things, just like now. Poverty was the feature of both eras. Maybe at different scales. Communities were divided by social and economic status.

Suad grew up like the other girls. The way she dressed or observed the norm was not dissimilar. For those around Suad, they saw her as a sensitive and responsible girl. They trusted her with their lives.

From an early age, Suad realised she physically lived among people, laughed the way they did, but cried in her own way.

Unfortunately, these characteristics were not without a heavy burden for her to take and a great cost to pay.

She was admired by the boys who looked at her with different lenses. The girls felt jealous. They intentionally made her life difficult.

Her cousin felt there was nothing to worry about, as she would be his future wife, in accordance with their strong traditions. Everyone blessed this unwritten deal. He was devoted to her father, with no boy around. He worked with him in the field and looked after their affairs. All that had gone when he sought his uncle's permission to marry Suad.

To his great dismay, she turned him down. The father believed he was obliged to seek his daughter's approval according to his religion. He made his views clear not to oppress or force her in making any decision. She had chosen not to marry her cousin. He was saddened by this unexpected shock.

Following that decision, the cousin distanced himself from them. In no time, he married a very young girl. He had a good life apart from the fact that he was troubled by an unexplained burden. From time to time he became agitated. He didn't share his worries with his wife, neither did she press him. Unfortunately, his wife didn't know that he lived loyal to a shadow of another woman.

Suad, along with her family, struggled because of her refusal to marry her cousin. As a result, she matured quickly. Regardless of the fact that she decided her fate, neither she, nor her mother had a say in most of the other family affairs. From time to time Sakina felt guilty giving birth to Suad.

Life changed rapidly for the family the day they heard loud noises outside their home. The men were carrying their father's body. He slipped and fell into the well. His life was ended in a dark wet place trying to support his family with no social support or inheritance of any kind.

The husband of the eldest daughter stepped up. He took care of the two families. The atmosphere was filled with uncertainty. The time moved slowly, if not stood still. Their days were unpredictable. They were always unsure of what to expect next.

As the years passed by quickly, the routine was the same till that day when the head of the family suddenly passed away. His time had come.

The house stood still with no emotion. As the situation became darker, the older sister followed her late husband's footsteps. She took the responsibility. For the first time in her life, she took a manual job in a nearby clinic, to support her family.

The other sister decided to follow her sister's path as their income was tight whilst their needs were growing. Their mother had a cocktail of medical conditions. They were in need of every penny to prevent her health deteriorating.

The third sister got married. Together with her husband, she moved away. From time to time she sent money to support the family.

Saud felt lonely. She didn't see a respectful, prosperous future for her there. She opened up to her sister who left a long time ago.

Soon after, she was alone in a huge, fast train. Saud started to draw a picture in her mind of a strange place with mysterious, weird people. She dreamt of being more well off than she was back home. The reality surprised her beyond any expectation. It was ridiculously pricey there. Her sister was unable to help or take her in. Therefore, her dream of a better life and sending money to the family evaporated in her early days.

It was not so easy for her to integrate. She couldn't wear the same clothes from back home. To just buy acceptable clothes, she needed a lot of money, which she couldn't afford.

Suad decided to study and work at the same time. She joined a special school which helped those with a low level of education. The harsh reality was that, she could only afford to live in the school's accommodation. They were allowed to work for specific companies in accordance with the school's rules. Some of their income was deducted by the Authority to cover their expenses. She did well in the school, which got her a scholarship to join the nearby college. She moved to a new student accommodation. She also had to pay and cover her expenses.

Weeks passed faster than expected. She found it harder to get used to the new life in the college. She started to feel low most of the time as she failed to be part of her new environment.

Steadily she started to change. She tried hard to become, speak, dress like a city girl. She thought she gained unlimited freedom. However, unexpectedly, she discovered that there was a powerful part inside her, that constantly restricted her choices. Most of the time she was very annoyed and tried hard to get rid of it. For whatever reason, she failed to silence it.

One of her colleagues, Osman, had captured her vulnerability. He planned carefully to take advantage of this fragile country girl, who had a boiling volcano inside her. "You can easily spot that she is naïve," he praised himself.

Back home, girls were not good with relationships. The community does not accept open love stories. Although it was obvious to outsiders that she was an intelligent woman, she struggled to differentiate between the genuine and false feelings. This was the problem that destroyed her, in a very different setting.

Osman perfectly imitated the ideal lover. In fact, he was the opposite to her in all aspects: his dreams, way of thinking and aspirations.

At the start of their relationship, she enjoyed the courtesy and fondness he showed. Even her cousin who loved her profoundly, had fallen short of what she was experiencing now.

Osman took her to unfamiliar, elegant places. He treated her to very nice luxurious food, which she never knew existed.

When Osman felt she was relaxed in his companionship, he started to negatively comment on her taste for clothes and hair style. She thought that was the worst but he made much more insensitive remarks and advances. He easily managed to lure her and always got the thumbs-up. She didn't know if he would ever stop.

The minute she thought that was all, he took pictures of them in odd places and positions. In spite of feeling intimidated, Suad was unable to hold herself back.

After that, she started to deliberately avoid him, leaving the premises as soon as lessons had finished.

"The only mistake I made was following my desire to explore new adventures, putting my trust in a total stranger. I don't know whether it is too late to amend things."

Guessing her intentions, Osman had carefully planned his coming steps. He was just like a spider that attractively crafted its web. The moment a fly set a foot on; it was trapped.

Osman went too far that night. She shouted "no" into an indifferent ear. Her vocal cords were smashed by the intensity of feeling guilty. She was paralysed by the heavy weight over her.

Following that dark night, he created and shared a horrible profile. He called it "Our Sweet Experiences", to leave her with no option but to stay under his command. Who knows, maybe this experience was his opportunity to start a successful business!

She was surrounded by laughing eyes, winks and whispers. The girls distanced themselves from her. The boys called her horrible names. The shameful pictures were added to the galleries of all smart phones, leaving her twisted inside.

"How could I live with that? How can I trust anyone anymore? I didn't even recognise my deep-rooted self.

"I admit I enjoyed his advances at the time, ignoring the fact that they didn't seem right. I think he must have added alcohol to my drinks. I don't remember how I was able to get rid of the image of my family which kept me safe?

"How dare I forget the many hands, passions and hearts that once surrounded me? How dare I forget the body of my father who ended up in a dark hole in the ground to provide a good life for us?"

Suicidal thoughts repeatedly crossed her mind.

"No," she screamed, "I have the right to live, to enjoy life. It is my time." She stopped suddenly, as the sound of the aggressive bangs of the dark clouds attacking each other broke the silence of the room. The bright light from the interaction, mixed with the heavy tears of the sky, created a non-sympathetic scene to what was happening inside.

Suad remembered what she had gone through, her many difficulties and the bitter experiences, that crushed her to nothing. At that horrible time, she lost her self-respect as well as the trust put on her by her family, before her community. That had been her biggest regret.

Suad slipped into a deep sleep after another life was created. This time there was no father waiting anxiously at the outer side of the room's door, holding his dear *Sibha*.

However, she learnt valuable lessons which she passed onto the girls in the village. She taught them how to stand up and believe in themselves, no matter how hard it might be. She reminded them to always listen to that part inside them which would guide them when they were most in need. Her most valuable advice was not to surrender even if they were surrounded by discontent, guilt, defeat, pain or distress.

Suad accomplished many great achievements, in very challenging circumstances. She used her story to coach the many girls who could have followed her deadly path.

It is the forgotten "watchdog" that rescued her from the huge losses.

Difficult Choices

Born without meeting her parents. Her family was involved in an accident by an overworked, sleepy and uninsured lorry driver. They were on their way to hospital to award the world with a new member. The father was announced dead at the scene. The mother was bleeding all the way to the theatre. Sadly, she never lived to hold her baby.

This was how Bisi arrived into the world. Auntie Harper and her husband Ginji adopted her and her brother Patel. They gave them all their attention. The couple couldn't have children of their own. They became to them "the real parents". The children called them Mum and Dad.

Harper baked bread or doughnuts depending on the availability of the ingredients. It also depended on the orders made the day before. Her customers were usually busy families who had no time for baking.

Both were very happy that the children didn't complain about the standard of living they provided. It was considered good compared with other dwellings in the area.

Patel was supported in education all along. His sister learnt from him, as was the case for many girls in the village. She sat at his feet when he was doing his homework. Every day, she woke up early to help their mother make breakfast for him. Bisi loved preparing his bag each morning and waving goodbye every single day. At noon, she was the first to welcome him home. Usually, she washed his uniform. Her favourite part was ironing his clothes to perfection. She left no crease intact.

Sometimes he took his sister for a walk to break the boredom which he noticed on her face. It was obvious that as much as Bisi, Harper was very proud of him. They watched him growing up. Both had the ideal picture of him in their minds.

Despite his busy schedule, he always socialised with the boys in the evenings playing football, sharing experiences and enjoying other activities.

Above all, he never let his family down. He was a flawless helper for Ginji, the same as for the entire neighbourhood. He never turned his back on someone in need.

When he joined the high school, he had to travel to the city. There was no such facility at home. He took his limited baggage including food, which was prepared for him, before heading off.

It was another life for him which was totally different from the current one. Meanwhile, his sister started to make national dresses. She sold them mainly to girls, to raise additional money for Patel. Bisi had a touch of creativity which placed her products in high demand. Her work had paid off. She made a respectable income. Boys' requests soon dominated her list, for her unusual contemporary designs. Traditionally, this job was done by older folks.

"I want Patel to be the best," she said. So, she carefully designed, one-off styles for him.

At home, she counted the days to the holiday breaks. To her disappointment, on his last visit, she observed he was a bit distant.

He started to dislike their national costumes. Instead he dressed in bizarre, ridiculous outfits. His taste was disapproved of by all. The way he spoke had changed. He was not interested in socialising with the boys anymore. He chose to leave so quickly. Bisi didn't complain to a soul. Just felt very sad. Everyone could see the hidden disappointment in the eyes of his parents.

The community gave up on him as they felt he looked down at them. The local girls stopped mentioning his name as they used to do. In the past they hailed him as their exemplar. Now they witnessed him falling from his horse. This was deemed a catastrophic ending for any hero. It was so painful for all to observe how his armour had been stolen by the city. This was not the case for him, judging by the fact that he stopped recognising their holy festivals. Even, he didn't care about his people anymore. He might have been ashamed of their purity or the integrity of their simple life. The new place had different inducing priorities.

Bisi didn't approve of his attitude at any point. Despite the gloom surrounding his behaviour, including his disloyalty, she carried on sending him money anyway.

Patel only sent letters if he needed more money. He didn't acknowledge receipt of what they had sent. He took it as their obligation to do so.

To comfort her parents, Bisi kept telling them Patel sent his regards and appreciation.

Deep down Bisi hoped that one day he would come back to his senses. She took it as just a phase in his life, which would soon disappear. Without a shade of hesitation, she continued to offer him advice.

Their parents were no longer able to provide for them as before. It seemed Patel was not interested in how they coped. They expected him to come back after finishing high school, the recognised level for boy's education, following which young men took on family responsibilities. This had not happened with Patel.

People noticed that the sparkle died in Bisi's eyes as she became preoccupied. They guessed she might have set herself up to believe Patel would put things right, which never materialised.

The whole village soon discarded him.

Harper was suffering in silence. Her health rapidly declined. Bisi wrote to Patel asking if he could have them for a short time to see the doctors. The local clinics were not functioning. Other families, whose boys took the same route, arranged for them to come to see the doctors. Bisi and her mother gave up as they hadn't heard from Patel.

Harper's heart stopped beating with no regret of what she had done for him. Even then, he didn't bother to send a message of condolence.

Bisi worked as a child minder with one of the well-off families, in addition to sewing. After a long period of hesitation, she stopped sending money to her brother. Instead, she put some money aside, just in case.

At this crucial time, the elders of the village met to discuss an issue which was very important to them. They decided that the Chief's son, Fouad, had to marry Bisi. Deep inside she welcomed the move. What bothered her was the fact that Fouad was also dreaming of moving far away.

Ginji encouraged Bisi to go, assuring her that he would be fine. She could see his tiny body shaking, like a leaf in the open battering a strong gale.

She was also aware how strongly Fouad wanted to leave the village behind. Looking at him she only saw her brother, who swapped his family and community with a dream.

She anticipated that Fouad would follow her brother's footsteps. He could easily give up on her with no sense of guilt whatsoever. She imagined him walking over her father's weak body, as an aisle, on his and the city's wedding day.

Bisi was torn between two thoughts. Either she leaves the village unknowing who would look after her father or lose her only chance to be happy and have her own family. "I deserve to be happy." Many thoughts crossed her mind.

Bisi felt she had given a lot to avoid disappointing her family. She might have sacrificed her happiness, but it was hard to imagine how her father would have coped if she had gone. She knew her brother's actions killed their father inside, but as expected, he always pretended to be okay for her sake.

"He looked after us and never complained or openly acknowledged his agony, despite the fact that Harper and I knew he was dead inside. He didn't even shed a tear or show if he was annoyed," she thought loudly.

"I can't do the same to him, walk over his pain." She decided to discuss her worries with Fouad. She convinced herself that he would understand.

With apparent unease, she spoke to him. At least she felt relieved. This was the first time ever Bisi shared her emotions with anyone. She begged him to stay.

Fouad kept talking about their future adventures with the same level of enthusiasm. It seemed as if he hadn't listened to a word she said.

"What about taking Dad with us then?" She asked again with a broken feeling inside. It was not long before his happy face had totally changed.

Although, she also fancied going to a new place, the continuous cough of her father brought her back to reality. She went to her father's room, cuddled him like he did when she was as tiny as his warm hands. Her soul reached out to his, seeking his advice, as she felt guilty for the disloyal thoughts. She recalled that he hadn't let her or her brother down when they were most in need. "How dare I just think even for a second to leave?" She took a deep breath, entered the other room where Fouad was still dreaming about the future. With no hesitancy or second thoughts, she softly whispered, looking directly into his eyes, "Fouad, can you please close the outer door behind you." She proudly smiled.

The next day, at the exact time when Fouad left, her father's heartbeats stopped, allowing his spirit to float freely. His body was put to rest, side by side with his wife's.

The one thing Bisi didn't regret was this decision.

Al-dahabaya

The Incredible Domestic Servant

The Birth of a Piece of Gold

Al-dahabaya, the tiny piece of gold, was confirmed as the official name for the newly born girl on her seventh day. Her mother chose this name to show how dearly she appreciated her baby, who was far too underweight.

A series of events took place to celebrate the arrival of the new citizen and mark the increase in the tribe's numbers. Big families were appreciated. They held women only events. Men attended the naming ceremony only. They were seated separately, according to the traditions.

In that culture, women were mostly appreciated for their beauty and the level of their attractiveness. Therefore, it was no wonder they were pigeonholed more or less by their taste for jewellery, costumes and perfumes, the same as the modern beauty contestant and fashions shows.

A week before Al-dahabaya's arrival, women started the preparations by looking after their bodies and hair. They organised sessions of aroma saunas and sandalwood treatments, which were mainly for married women.

They also decorated their hands and feet, using a special plant, Henna. A dark, shiny tan would remain after they had washed off the Henna, leaving an eye-catching authentic artwork. The depth of the colour varied in different communities, depending on the length of time it was left on or the type of the Henna they used. It would stay for many weeks before it faded away, to be repeated with different designs.

Observation: Many years after, with the change of life style, the henna plant was replaced by chemical dyes, resulting in the spread of allergic reactions.

During the events they executed a non-official beauty fashion show, which presented opportunities for families to choose brides for their unmarried sons, brothers and male relatives. The events were considered a vital part of the dominating arranged marriage culture.

The ceremonies were music to the ears of the women beauticians, as their customers were noticed.

The gatherings also presented an opportunity for business women, who were specialised in marriage matching, to flourish.

Observation: In a different world, this culture had been replicated and modernised in line with the digital revolution. These business women, were replaced by digital alternatives, the dating sites.

On the night before the delivery, the neighbours arrived to dress the beds in all the rooms, where the guests would sit. Furnishing rooms in that way was the common feature in most of the houses. They also brought "Bumbars" which were small seats with leather or special dried plants woven on the top, to accommodate additional guests.

Early morning after the baby was born, the women in charge brought a small pedestal bowl with fragrant burning coal that filled the room with a distinctive scent. This was used as a way to destroy the malicious eye, which they believed could cause catastrophes. The house was then completed, ready to welcome guests.

The new mum rested on a big wooden bed with four poles. The women hung a mesh curtain around the bed to deter flies and mosquitos from disturbing the mother-baby moments, when they bond during breastfeeding sessions. They covered them with a coloured, perfumed, silky quilt. It had different stripes, which were magnificently integrated, creating a soothing feel for both.

The red stripes symbolised the blood during the process of giving birth, representing the eternal bond between them. The brown, together with the green colour, reflected the life-giving earth. The yellow and orange reminded the mother of the sunset and sunrise, which meant a happy progress in life. The blue colour imitated a pure spirit, just like a stream, which kindly invited you to dive deep into its heart. Last, but not least, the silver colour mirrored a soothing night, that was visited by happy lights from the full moon.

All unmarried women or those who had no children brought symbolic gifts for the baby. They also offered to help the new mum and to carry out any duties assigned to them. Each one whispered a wish to Al-dahabaya, which was never revealed.

The help included, changing as well as washing the baby's nappies, which were made from cotton as the weather was extremely dry and hot. This way new-borns would not suffer from rashes or discomfort. In addition, reusable nappies were far more affordable. Above all they would contribute to preserving the environment.

For the first two weeks after giving birth, the closest neighbours cooked special dishes for the mother. This voluntary gesture was fulfilled as if it was a duty. It reflected the collective valued generosity within their community.

The foundation of these traditions was based on the belief that making innocent babies happy, brings blessings to those who were kind to them.

Al-dahabaya's Childhood

Al-dahabaya had an angelic look peacefully sleeping in the rocking cot besides her mother's bed. From time to time a gentle smile appeared on her little face as if an angel had visited her. This smile represented a divine hint that God is blessing both.

At her naming ceremony, each woman in the neighbourhood brought a dish to share with everyone. Some women could only afford to bring juices, dates, pastries or tea, instead of the expected dish. Still they were highly appreciated. No one but the household people would know who brought what. They never talked about anyone's contribution in accordance with the saying "what happens in the house, stays in the house".

On the morning of the naming day a male choir was seated outside the house under a decorated marquee. The men performed religious routines which were very beautiful and spiritual. They were synchronised with the strong drum's rhythms.

They attracted the attention of the women who were gathered at the other side of the wall that surrounded the house. The performance created a very emotional and inspiring environment, which offered a unity against evil.

After they had breakfast, drank tea or coffee, the men left.

For women the fun had just started. The most popular act amongst the female guests, was the performance of the pumpkin's singing group. This was a traditional musical entertainment, performed by elderly women.

To start with, they filled a big container with water, then immersed several halves of dried pumpkins which immediately floated. Using special canes, they gently hit them repeatedly in a certain order. The pumpkins vibrated creating diverse, remarkable and harmonised soft tunes.

Girls, together with women, performed collective or individual dances to the rhythm of the many songs. The preferred one was the "peace pigeon". Women dancers dressed in national, bright, silky white costumes. It gave the impression that it just loosely hanged from the head and shoulders. It just rested on their body in complete harmony.

The other dance that was loved was the sword dance. It represented the courage of women. The rhythmic movements reflected the body when riding a horse or a camel.

The youngest girls demonstrated modern routines. They particularly captured the eyes of the attending mothers of grown up men.

When dusk arrived, women prayed together for the baby to be good for their parents, family, neighbours and the entire village. They also prayed for the mother to be healthy enough to offer rich milk for her baby girl.

When the ceremony finished, every woman collected her belongings. The singers poured water all over the yard, wishing them both a peaceful, joyful life. Water was regarded as a holy gift to clean the house of any intended or unintended nasty act or wish of hate.

The eldest group guided the guests out of the house singing a special song. They walked in a circle seven times to mark every day since Al-dahabaya was born. Then, they sang a song which was specially written for her. The alphabet of her name, would be used to positively describe the life ahead of her and wish her well.

When the sun's rays faded, they looked towards the yellow-reddish ball. Each one took a few steps forward, then suddenly stopped singing. After a short time of silence, they turned towards the house. This was a respectful gesture, appealing to God to guide the family through darkness during life.

After that holy moment, women walked in different directions. They were filled with happiness, as the extended family showed appreciation for what they had done.

The distant cry of the baby declared that she was healthy, as she successfully managed to expand her lungs, allowing the cry to reach out far beyond her cot.

Until the baby was forty days old, the family members continued to visit regularly to offer their help. The mother was not allowed to go out. Sometimes the neighbours join in, till the mother is able to take control of her new situation and the baby strong enough to face the world around.

On the fortieth day, another gathering took place. All guests, and family members, accompanied the mother and baby to the river. The mother washed her face and the baby's. All those who accompanied them would do the same. They considered this visit as a holy introduction of the baby to life outside the safe womb.

The village continued vibrating with excitement again and again, whenever, another woman gave birth.

Message to the Reader: People may undermine the power of culture and beliefs; however, these communities lived a relatively simple and happy life, with no setback by material demands.

People may think their quality of life was poor. However, those communities might not have such desires to depend on drugs, alcohol or other means to feel good about themselves and their lives.

I guess it wasn't the norm for young people to end their lives, harm themselves or depend on mental health services, within the above-mentioned communities.

Al-dahabaya's Journey for Survival

Many years after Al-dahabaya's birth, the village suffered from a severe drought. The rainy season was replaced by intensely hot months, which continued all year long. As a result, farming had vanished taking with it the livestock. People were forced to migrate just to live. The most distressing thing was that they had to surrender their community identity.

A large number of people were lost during the unplanned trips to grab a slice of a normal life. Families were scattered all over the routes. Some of the strongest people, mainly young men, were able to catch non-stopping trucks. They jumped and hung on the rails at the side of the lorry for a considerable length of time. Many travelled aimlessly on foot, unaware of their fate.

Little boys, together with girls, were begging on the roads. Some of them were picked up by travellers' cars, to the unknown, others were taken by motorbikes.

The luckiest ones found work in the many basic cafés which were scattered by the road sides. A few took jobs at hubs that handled goods. What they received in exchange was an insignificant amount of money.

That road was full of traffic, as sole traders commissioned drivers to distribute their stocks. They mainly used that route, because it connected the cities across the region, with the harbour.

Al-dahabaya was around twelve, when her village fell apart. Her family lost their cattle as they were unable to carry on farming. They sold their farm to a wealthy trader.

She was separated from her family. She struggled as did the rest of the children. She walked towards the nearest town, accompanied by two friends. The weather was harsh. The temperature was extremely high during the day. The night may have seemed cooler, with a drop of only three degrees. They slept on dried grass when the darkness dressed the roads. Some of the car drivers sympathised with the scene and gave them bread, water and some change.

A new type of business was born out of this situation. Agents that provide domestic help was established. Young girls, who were scattered all over, were recruited as domestic workers. They went to the areas which flourished around the road.

One of the conditions was that families who needed the service, should allow the recruits to live with them. This was not a problem for many wealthy families as the households in general were big, with huge yards that surrounded the buildings. Most of them had small rooms for workers.

The gardener might have used the same space for his break, whilst the girls were cleaning the main residence. This arrangement could easily put them at risk, but was the best at the time.

They didn't have a choice or an alternative.

Al-dahabaya was one of the relatively lucky girls who found such a job.

The New Life

Al-dahabaya was taken to work with a family in the capital. The house and the surrounding areas were very different to where her family lived. She was overwhelmed by the huge villas, cars, cooling systems together with varieties of food and fruits. She was even taken aback by dinner sets, cups and saucers in addition to other things. She hadn't seen what is called *cutlery* before. She was captivated by how the women dressed. For her it was like being reborn in heaven.

She had no contract. She had to do whatever was asked of her at any time. Her working hours had no limits. She only had one day off per week, but she was not allowed to sleep out on any day. Logically, if she were at the house on her day off, she would not refuse to help, the same as she would do at her family home.

Her day would usually start at five in the morning by preparing the tea and helping the kids dress for school. In addition to cleaning all the huge rooms, verandas and bathrooms, she also had to clean the limitless yard. It posed a challenge for her. Obviously, she couldn't use the vacuum cleaner there. Al-dahabaya was impressed when they introduced this gadget to her, when she started this job. It took her ages to become friends with it. The most she feared was using any electrical item.

In the afternoon she would help the wife with cooking, washing as well as ironing the clothes. When the family members returned home, Al-dahabaya would bring in the food, after assisting the children to change.

She also should accommodate and serve the guests who could come at any time of the day. To add to that there were the nitty gritty trivial jobs in between.

She was the last to eat. Most of the time, it was the left overs. By the time she hit the bed, understandably she was exceptionally exhausted.

As life went by, Al-dahabaya felt happier, though homesick. What usually triggered this reaction was when she saw the whole family sitting together under the stars, laughing with joy. In contrast, she didn't know where her mother, father or her siblings were. At night she cried till she fell asleep. In the morning the cycle would start again.

Al-dahabaya had never talked over anyone in the house, complained or used anything without permission. She went beyond her responsibilities to make the children happy. She remembered that warm sensation from her childhood when she was around them.

Soon enough the family recognised her outstanding manner. They started to treat her with respect, which was unusual in these circumstances. The children were attached to her to the extent that they repeatedly offered to help. They trusted her with their secrets. Sometimes their mother got annoyed that her kids confided with a worker, not with her. As a result of such deliberation with herself, her mood could change drastically. At other times, she became harsh, communicating with Al-dahabaya for no obvious reason. She was quick to calm down. However, no apology was ever offered. Al-dahabaya got used to that, which was not in any way compared to what other domestic servants experienced.

With the help of the girls, she learnt to write and read together with new skills. Their mother knew nothing about this arrangement.

The mother gave Al-dahabaya used clothes. Mostly they were not wanted, as they were out of fashion. Some of the dresses needed adjustment. In return, she made it a habit to always treat the girls, when they accompanied her to local shops.

She put some money aside for unexpected eventualities. Her big dream was to be reunited with her family, who would need her support under the circumstances.

Years went by with no noticeable changes. Her routine was the same, apart from a little rise in her salary.

Once, she opened up to the mother about her intentions. In her mind, there was a very special memory; her mother was a Henna specialist. Her talent was recognised beyond their village. Al-dahabaya wanted to do something to keep this memory alive. She was convinced this would make her mother happy, as much as proud.

Therefore, she became deeply engulfed in persistent thoughts about what she wanted to do.

One morning, during their discussion, Al-dahabaya started to cry. The lady of the house hesitantly hugged her tight, as if she was one of her girls. That moment took her back, across the years, to her childhood imagining the cuddle was from her mother. Despite it being genuinely warm, the feel, for her was different.

A couple of days later, the mother offered her their garage to start her project. The children noticed that Al-dahabaya was repeatedly absent from the house. They just didn't question it. Their Mum sometimes asked them to do some work, which was usually covered by Al-dahabaya. They shrugged their shoulders and just went with it.

It seemed strange that Al-dahabaya asked the children to help her clean the garage. They didn't guess what she was up to but blindly followed her.

The Reward

The whole family including the mother, were shocked by the transformation of the unused garage to a luxurious beauty salon. It was hard to believe, all that was done by her single-handedly.

The *deco* and the Henna design samples were imaginative. They instigated inspiring stories that took you to infinity. The first customer was the lady of the house, who was then followed by many sophisticated ladies.

She recommended a trustful replacement for the family. She had known that girl for a long time. They both started their journey out of their village on foot, till they were rescued by a van driver. He introduced them to their first ever employment, as domestic servants. Since then, they continued to socialise during their days off.

The beauty salon became well known amongst the rich dignitaries of the society. It expanded very quickly and occupied the heart of the business community. Al-dahabaya employed talented women to run the many branches which opened across the city. She bought herself a respectful house and moved into it.

Al-dahabaya kept in touch with the family, sharing with them her plans for the future. Occasionally, she came to visit them, at any time. She was well served as a guest.

She had another passionate idea that popped up from the past, which she felt obliged to accomplish. She opened two free bed and breakfast accommodations for young girls. They were located on the same road, which once she walked along unsure where she would end, and how.

When she travelled back, she found the scene had not changed a lot. She saw herself in every single girl who was zigzagging on that road to avoid being run over. She experienced the same feelings that consumed her, long ago, taking that journey to nowhere. The cold reminded her of her dress which barely covered her body. It looked like a mesh rather than a dress. Her shoes trailed her tiny feet, causing her to trip over.

The horns of the slowly moving lorries were still there squeaking when children suddenly crossed the road in a hurry to get a piece of bread or a bottle of water. She remembered all of it. She was paralysed and unable to move, due to the weight of the memories. She just sat down on the side of the road and threw up. People gathered around her. Many onlookers offered her water in dirty glasses.

"Are you okay?"

"Yes, but they were not."

"Who are they?"

"Me and the others."

"She needs a doctor."

"I don't. They do. Where are their parents and mine?"

"How many could I help?

Ten ... twelve? Who will help the rest?"

"She lost consciousness," one of the people shouted louder. "Is there any medic?"

"I am a nurse."

When she opened her eyes, in the hospital, the family she worked for, were surrounding her. She always kept their address in her bag.

That was the first time she spoke about her lost family.

A couple of months after, she opened a third bed and breakfast for more migrating girls. The family helped her set up an agency to help the girls pursue a brighter future.

With the family's advice, she organised another agency to help families separated through famine and other disasters, to find one another again.

"I was helped to get back my life!"

To test how successful this could be, she tasked them to find her family.

And ... they succeeded!

Daisy and Jack

Daisy and Jack were the same age kids, whose families were neighbours. They created their own sanctuary where they shared their true views, worries, emotions and aspirations without pretence or judgment.

They went through and were affected by a similar situation which perfectly fits with the psychological or physical child abuse definition. Their horrific experience included some sexual abuse from those who were supposed to guard them.

Both felt side-lined and scared as they were severely punished at home for what would be normal behaviour for their age. This was clearly reflected in their conduct at school. Initially, they were laughed at by fellow children. Then they were called names, such as "chicken" which was a huge deal for innocent children. The experience that totally changed them was the repeated physical attacks.

In response, they created inexplicable nicknames for themselves, the Brave King and Queen of the Fearfulness. The names were unwitting exhibits of conflicting feelings they both experienced at home and school at the same time.

Soon after, their behaviour changed. They became violent towards everybody. Teachers failed to see beyond their unacceptable performance.

With time, Daisy developed an extremely reckless attitude. She adopted an inconsiderate behaviour. She became indifferent to all circumstances including the way she ended her own life.

Gradually, Jack became aggressive at school. He gained a false respect from his frightened classmates. This resulted in him becoming an unreachable figure. In the process of seeking respect, he turned into a monster. His teachers implemented all known theories to reform him, without success. He continued to be rude to them. Eventually they gave up on him especially as his family was not so keen.

At times, he felt as if he was split in two halves with different personalities. He found it hard to keep his school persona flowing beyond the school gates. Sometimes he locked himself in the loo for the whole break time. None of his alleged mates dared to talk him out, because they didn't know the consequences. They were unable to report him to the teachers either, fearing they may be punished or expelled from his protection privilege. At the very least, they were freaked out by the thought they might be exposed to his cruel revenge.

He lived two different lives, the scared child at home and the scary monster at school.

Jack's Dad sensed what his son was going through. No doubt, he lived each moment of his son's silent suffering. Sadly, he could not help his boy, as he had no say in family affairs. His wife's family were well off, compared to his. They were controlling his and Jack's lives.

Inside, he knew he had let him down, unable to safeguard him from the harsh punishment he repeatedly faced. Unfortunately, he couldn't stand up for his own reputation let alone his child's. His hands were tied.

Although he loved Jack dearly, he was uncomfortable being around him. His prime agony was that Jack would be in the same situation.

He just enjoyed the fact that Jack was the only one in the family who understood and sympathised with him. He believed in his kindness, whilst all others saw his gentle nature as his greatest weakness. Jack appreciated him regardless.

With time Jack and Daisy turned teenagers. Life dispersed them in different walks, taking with them each other's secrets.

Jack and his son Dawood

Jack had his own kids. Unpredictably, he used all kinds of harsh punishments, wanting to believe he made his boy, Dawood, stronger. He ignored his son's look which reminded him of his own heartfelt disappointment a long time ago. He lived with that, to keep Dawood away from the need to create his own world with a neighbour's daughter. Categorically, he did not want him to seek comfort from a little girl, as he once did.

In response to his father's extreme stance combined with his own frustration, Dawood didn't seek comfort from a little girl but owned a sharp knife and a bottle of acid.

The situation later got out of hand, at some sad point. Only time will tell whether Dawood's off-spring will end up on the same path, moulding a violent non-stopping generation.

Daisy and her daughter Aml

As far as Daisy was concerned, she instinctively turned her unresponsive behaviour into a systematic self-destructive mind-set. Her attitude affected those around her. She only saw evil in their eyes. She felt the failure grasping her by the throat whilst her brain responses were totally frozen.

She started to hear whispers that turns into screams, roars, cries, then silence to start again. She behaved according to the flux of impulses which timed with the moment of the cycle. To be more precise, Daisy turned into a thick-hearted, cruel creature. She gradually became violent both verbally and physically, with a poisoned intellect. Hatred blinded her. She isolated herself from everybody around.

She left her family house young, without a trace. She deliberately moved to another area far from home. With intent, she cut off any contact with them. Her family reported her a missing person. They promised a huge sum for any useful information. Later she was

assumed to be dead. Her family grieved for a long tim
many things, when it was too late.

Soon after, Daisy found herself in a critical situa
brutal territorial gangsters. They targeted vulnerable
who were forced to live in the shadow outside the so
streets.

In the beginning she considered leaving. Eventuall
any idea which might release her from the agony she
for a long time.

She started a new life with a buzz, having many br
call themselves, including admirers. Soon enough she
hand over those who joined long before her. This
position was not earned because of her charm, it was
female members were recruited to gang communiti
were regarded as a liability. Nobody knew why.

She hugged and was being hugged. They led her to
whatever she dreamt of, feeling empowered. She
many loved her because they saw her as a pretty, stro

Before she started to enjoy her new status, she di
such circumstances, the concept of relationships
survival instinct. The version of human need to be
option. Therefore, her relationships started to droj
in pain.

Daisy became lonely and miserable, but shov
backing down or seeking help.

The drop of her relationship brought back to
memory. It was a war, as she saw it then, against
whom the farmer saw as outsiders. They used a
pesticides to conserve the survival of their crops.

So, the beetles dropped one by one, the same as
She understood now, the consequence of using t
more far reaching than she imagined. It affected
who suffered allergies, contaminated the water
polluting the environment.

She looked deeply at both occurrences, to find those in charge didn't care, as far as their residence, cars and offices were environmentally friendly. Equally, those in power didn't care about those forced to join gangs, as long as their own children were safe.

The connection between the fall of Daisy's relationships and the fall of the beetles, could have been differently handled.

Daisy became pregnant, without knowing who the father was. When she was about to give birth, she was dropped at the hospital gate. She gave birth to a beautiful daughter, Aml, which means hope. Unfortunately, she would never know her roots.

Social services looked after Daisy and her baby. They offered her small room in a hostel. They assigned a social worker to help her when needed.

Daisy developed a severe anxiety following the birth of her child. was not picked up by her social worker. She mistakenly took it as part of her aggressive behaviour.

Daisy started to have nightmares as she saw her reflection in her daughter's tiny face. She also experienced a new different feeling which she didn't recognise. She was torn between the new and wrong feeling of motherhood and the inner urge to take revenge from her past.

No one guessed that Daisy would never hit her baby girl. She defied all expectations. Whenever the baby cried, she sat helpless on the corner holding her head between her knees. She just froze and stayed still, until the baby stopped crying or slipped into a deep nap.

From lack of experience, one day Daisy locked Aml in the room to to the shop to buy nappies. She was arrested for causing disturbances in the supermarket.

It didn't bother or cross her mind to tell them that her daughter was alone at home. Luckily enough the neighbours heard the continuous crying of the baby. Aml was cold, hungry, scared and wet, then rescued that day.

That was the last time Daisy saw her little girl. Her mind was always occupied by the thought of what became of her. She imagined her transformed into a monster. But soon she dismissed the

thought. She was full of hope that her tiny baby would find a stable home.

She couldn't accept the possibility of a worse scenario that her girl might face life alone after turning eighteen, with no future to look forward to. She dismissed the option that she might end up in one of the hostels, the way she had. The breaking point for her was thinking about Aml not knowing her family or her birthplace.

The Fate

On one dark day, a girl was orphaned as a mother under the name of Daisy threw herself out of a window above a busy road. There was no prospect that the speeding, packed traffic would miss her. An appeal was launched for the next of kin to come forward but that was the end of the effort.

Just around the corner that day a man called Jack was stabbed to death, shielding his son Dawood from being stabbed.

The son was arrested for possession of a large knife. Since then no one had heard about him.

A message for the Reader: Different circumstances, different experiences with the same consequence for many communities. Difficult questions need to be asked, even if there is no solution for whatever reason.

I wonder when the sorrow together with the regrets disappear and everyone stands nude in front of their conscience, what will be the cost? Then, who is to blame? Will there be any chance for rescue? I doubt it.

Who will we declare the loser? Will there have been any choices for reform or have they just been brushed away? Will social service's capacity be able to solve such problems? God knows.

The main question which still remains hanging over our heads is – how can we strike a balance between extremism, hatred, prejudice and the undesirable, on one hand, compared with tolerance, fairness, sensibility and last, but not least, moderation?

How many Jacks and Daisys are out there, calling to us to be rescued?

What you caught sight of, is not an unusual incidence. So, let us hope or think seriously of making it the last. Gang members were people just like us. Maybe, society has driven them out in our streets, leaving them to jump off the cliff's edge.

If only one person were pushed to join a gang, that is one person too many.

assumed to be dead. Her family grieved for a long time, regretting many things, when it was too late.

Soon after, Daisy found herself in a critical situation amongst brutal territorial gangsters. They targeted vulnerable young people, who were forced to live in the shadow outside the society, in many streets.

In the beginning she considered leaving. Eventually, she resisted any idea which might release her from the agony she had lived with for a long time.

She started a new life with a buzz, having many brothers, as they call themselves, including admirers. Soon enough she had the upper hand over those who joined long before her. This high-ranking position was not earned because of her charm, it was because fewer female members were recruited to gang communities. Maybe, they were regarded as a liability. Nobody knew why.

She hugged and was being hugged. They led her to believe she got whatever she dreamt of, feeling empowered. She started to think many loved her because they saw her as a pretty, strong, funny sister.

Before she started to enjoy her new status, she discovered that in such circumstances, the concept of relationships depends on the survival instinct. The version of human need to bond, was not an option. Therefore, her relationships started to drop off one by one, in pain.

Daisy became lonely and miserable, but showed no signs of backing down or seeking help.

The drop of her relationship brought back to mind a childhood memory. It was a war, as she saw it then, against innocent beetles whom the farmer saw as outsiders. They used a man-made rain of pesticides to conserve the survival of their crops.

So, the beetles dropped one by one, the same as her relationships. She understood now, the consequence of using the bug killer was more far reaching than she imagined. It affected some individuals who suffered allergies, contaminated the water resources besides polluting the environment.

She looked deeply at both occurrences, to find those in charge didn't care, as far as their residence, cars and offices were environmentally friendly. Equally, those in power didn't care about those forced to join gangs, as long as their own children were safe.

The connection between the fall of Daisy's relationships and the fall of the beetles, could have been differently handled.

Daisy became pregnant, without knowing who the father was. When she was about to give birth, she was dropped at the hospital gate. She gave birth to a beautiful daughter, Aml, which means hope. Unfortunately, she would never know her roots.

Social services looked after Daisy and her baby. They offered her a small room in a hostel. They assigned a social worker to help her when needed.

Daisy developed a severe anxiety following the birth of her child. It was not picked up by her social worker. She mistakenly took it as part of her aggressive behaviour.

Daisy started to have nightmares as she saw her reflection in her daughter's tiny face. She also experienced a new different feeling which she didn't recognise. She was torn between the new and strong feeling of motherhood and the inner urge to take revenge from her past.

No one guessed that Daisy would never hit her baby girl. She defied all expectations. Whenever the baby cried, she sat helpless on the corner holding her head between her knees. She just froze and stayed still, until the baby stopped crying or slipped into a deep nap.

From lack of experience, one day Daisy locked Aml in the room to go to the shop to buy nappies. She was arrested for causing disturbances in the supermarket.

It didn't bother or cross her mind to tell them that her daughter was alone at home. Luckily enough the neighbours heard the continuous crying of the baby. Aml was cold, hungry, scared and wet, when rescued that day.

That was the last time Daisy saw her little girl. Her mind was always occupied by the thought of what became of her. She imagined her transformed into a monster. But soon she dismissed the

Canary

Canary was a young mother to an eight-year girl and nine-year boy. She dedicated all her time to raise her children to the highest standard. She took them to school every day and made sure they were happy.

Canary provided all that they needed for their physical as well as psychological well-being. They lived on a very affluent street.

One day whilst looking at the TV, after preparing lunch, a breaking news was running at the bottom of the screen: **A boat has capsized ... A boat has capsized ... A boat has capsized ...**

Two bodies of an eight-year girl and nine-year boy were washed out on the bank of a river in a small, distant place. This happened when they tried to cross the river in an old, unsafe boat, which had no life jackets. Both were holding tight to school bags with their names and classes written on the front.

Canary's eyes filled with tears when she saw the picture of the incident displayed on the screen. It was the saddest image she had seen in all her life.

She ran towards the screen thinking they would come back to life, if she performed a mouth-to-mouth procedure. She placed her mouth on the screen and started blowing continuously, till her energy ran out. She fell on the floor breathing heavily.

The phone rang interrupting her midway of passing out. She dragged herself up holding onto the furniture to reach the forever-ringing phone.

"Ms Canary, your children are waiting for you in the Head Teacher's office." No reply was heard.

"Ms Canary, are you alright?"

A heavy weary sound came through the line. "Yes I am. Just ... I didn't sleep well last night. It seems I overslept. Sorry."

"That is fine, we will be waiting for you. See you soon."

The family arrived home. She didn't say a word, neither did the children. It was an unusual trip. This strange situation continued over lunch. The house was full of silence to the extent that you, the reader, could clearly hear the sound of their, as well as your own, heartbeats.

Both children noticed that their mother kept staring at them for some time, then turned her attention to the screen.

After a short time, they started running across the room passing in front of the television as they played hide and seek.

Unexpectedly, she shouted, "Be careful. The boat is sinking. Hold onto the rope. I am coming to rescue you." They stood still as she had never shouted at them before. They looked at each other briefly, then ran to their rooms.

The TV reporter stopped abruptly, as if sympathising with this frightened mother and the puzzled children. Canary was so sure he said sorry to those tiny bodies who should have been running in front of their mother's television, playing hide and seek. She didn't realise they might not even have a TV, judging by the boat which went under, taking them to a school in heaven.

Whenever, Canary was in front of the TV, she always saw her children's faces reflected on it. They seemed happy, laughing or messing about, just she noticed a hint of sadness misting their eyes. These moments continued for a long time.

Canary decided to go to a nearby place of worship, which she might not have chosen under different circumstances. She spent the whole morning looking up then down, crying, talking, smiling then shouting, with no one in the room. Canary felt outraged before she calmed down.

She prayed for all the children of the world to be safe, then quietly left the building feeling a great strength in her heart.

With a trembling hand she turned on the news. She crossed her arms over her chest, took a deep breath before she stared at the bottom of the screen. No breaking news was running across the screen. Instead, a programme about sailing was on. It grabbed her attention, taking her back years to when she was a young girl. The particulars of that special day invaded her memory, just like replaying a cassette on a recorder.

"Never seen a ferry as big as that. It reminded me of our town. I guess it has the same dimensions, though it was too high." That was what she said boarding a huge ferry during her geography lesson many years ago.

She smiled for the first time since the breaking news.

She recalled all the conversations and the valuable moments. She retold their story to the TV presenter.

"We were on a school journey across the ocean. The new teacher wanted us to have a life experience in addition to the boring geography lessons. We hated being glued to the classroom chairs with our body leaning on the hard-wooden desks.

I didn't enjoy geography lessons anyway. In contrast, I was fascinated by the visits to various places which, in my opinion, were more relevant and made sense of things.

Our teacher carefully chose charming places, that accurately mirrored each page of the geography book. Whilst the syllabus was unchanged, the way she approached it was distinctive. It was just amazing.

If the exam was based on these visits alone, I would have received the tops marks and left school at geography teacher's level. I wouldn't have struggled to just achieve the pass marks."

"Some of our class mates were sick during the journey," she continued. "They spent the whole time in their tiny cabins.

For me, it was a magical experience. I spent most nights sitting on the upper deck with my friend appreciating what we were witnessing. We were both stunned by the endless line where the water quietly moves to touch the sky, which embraced it all night. It seemed to us that the variation of the colour blue is endless. The sky was twinkling with natural light bulbs.

We spoke with very low tones so as not to disturb the glamour of the night. I always had an inclination to walk bare foot on the surface of the ocean. It looked so inviting with each drop of water perfectly fitted with the adjacent one.

We stared at the waves, hoping to catch a glimpse of the sea inhabitants dancing, then gliding across the top of the sea. I am sure they wouldn't disturb the soothing peaceful feel of the night. We never even felt the ship was vibrating."

Canary took a long breath, before continuing, "The only time I came to reality was when the siren signalled our arrival in a bay. We were allowed to get off. It was remarkable how each port on the way was totally different compared to the others.

We were asked to observe and find out as much as we could about the communities, customs, food, architecture, culture and folklore, in addition to any other matters of interest.

When we returned home, we were tasked with writing essays, poems or produce paintings based on our observations, for lessons which included geography, history, design and art, amongst others.

We were safe then. What happened now for the boat to sink? …"

Her children ran into the room quietly to find their Mum talking to the TV. "What a harsh world we live in? Is this what is called equality/inequality?

"Poor kids. Be happy in heaven, we lost control on earth." She wiped the tear from her cheeks. With an angelic soft tone, she whispered, "Tomorrow will be better. Rest in peace little angels."

She looked at her children, smiled and hugged them. She whispered, "You have a responsibility to better maintain our future. We failed terribly sacrificing our children to the water. God guard you. I will raise you to become fine human beings. You will end such breaking news."

Canary smiled widely, hugging both, "Sorry I scared you. I am sure you will understand one day. I was upset about a terrible thing, that happened far away from here, even I don't know where. I want you to always remember to be good and to stop the bad."

"Okay Mum." They crossed their little fingers with their Mum, "We promise. Don't cry."

A message to the Reader: I wonder, in which language did she feel, reacting to that horrific incident? What skin colour did she approve, to perform the "mouth to mouth" procedure?

Did the fact that the unsafe, old boat which was in the poorest area, far away, stop her tears flooding from an affluent street, where she lived?

In which culture had she felt the pain of those kids?

How to stop the war for power, that caused the boat to sink, whilst the world chose not to see, hear or feel?

When the South met the North

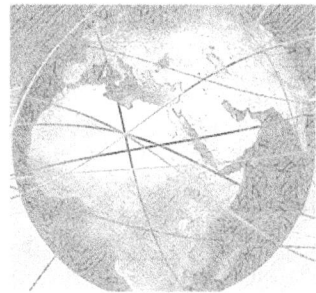

Ursula lived in one of the small cities in a Southern region of our planet. She was a researcher who specialised in the impact of social issues on communities.

Lisa was also a researcher in the same field but lived in the Northern region.

They both joined an open university, which had a rich diverse community, with different online groups. They met in one of them.

They started to work together when they discovered that they had almost the same ideas for their research. They decided to undertake a joint project entitled, "The Impact of Social Issues on Different Communities".

They chose a number of topics to study. They agreed to explore their impact on people's lives, in both the Northern and Southern regions. Then, they would compare the similarities and the differences and agree a conclusion. Their main goal was to find an untouched approach that could help change people's lives and attitudes for the better.

They both dreamt that the findings would offer a solution to bridge the gap between the similar, yet different, status quo.

They were convinced these issues had been spinning around for many departed centuries. The prime fear was that the trend would continue for years to come, if no actions were taken.

The findings surprised both of them when they shared their analysis, "Where has all the racism and hatred come from?" they whispered at the same time.

War and Disability

The researchers agreed war and disability as their first study. They switched on their computers and the camera, which allowed them to see each other and freely communicate. The two screens were divided into two halves, as the technology allowed.

On the left side of both screens, a long row of different people appeared. They had lost all, or part of, their legs, feet, fingers, arms or hands. They were singing:

"We are the world. We are the children. We were once happy, before guns were fired at us ..."

Ursula's warm tears made her face flush. Her heart started chasing the breathing muscles, that moved up and down, with great speed. This race caused irregular beats.

Lisa, on the other side, didn't take her eyes off the very long row and listened to their song. She was shivering because her tears were frozen on her cheeks. Her heart was also racing her breathing muscles' movements, that acted in the same way as Ursula's.

The girls' souls reached out to hug the fast-moving row, taking no notice of the disappearance of some or all of their limbs.

"It is just a miracle. Where did they find this energy to hold on? Maybe the bullets were catching up with them or their pride as humans prevailed their losses. Does it matter? They lost essential parts of themselves for no rational reason," Ursula whispered.

Ursula was overwhelmed by additional rows, that appeared on the right side of her screen. Lisa though, didn't have these rows. Her screen was blank.

They were not within the remit of their chosen subject for the first story of war and disability. Ursula was not surprised, contrary to Lisa, because she was aware of the massive issues in the south.

The first row on Ursula's screen, was a traditional, harmonised, beautiful but sad line of labourers. They were tired, miserable and desperate. They had been working very long hours, almost all day. The row was moving in-between lines of cotton plant, in a private estate. She heard the enchanted buds singing love songs, to make them happy. They miserably failed.

"For a long time, I believed that manual workers had better rights and conditions." She accepted that her assumption was wrong. Exploitation still rules.

Ursula explained to Lisa, her experience, when she was a young girl:

"I remember when I used to help my father picking cotton in a huge field. He was then just a suppressed cotton picker, one amongst many poor workers, in someone's titanic farm."

Looking back at the screen, she discovered there was another different row in a sugar cane field. "Oh my God, does slavery still exist?" She was overwhelmed. Lisa didn't see the new one either, but she could see how her friend was so sad, reacting to what was going on.

"Ursula, are you okay," said Lisa.

"Will be. That was cruel, as my grandfather used to say."

"Lisa could we have a break? These memories are painful."

"Of course, we can," replied Lisa.

Before they closed their computers, a voice from both screens interrupted them. "Aren't you going to explore the impact? That was the same. It even had impact on those who didn't live it, such as you Ursula. Besides, war shouldn't be by weapons only. What about economic conflict? You shouldn't consider the physical disabilities only. Goodbye." Their electronic advisors stopped talking but continued watching over them.

Both nodded in shock, but agreed.

They returned to their screens, to see if the rows of disabled people were still marching. They saw those in the first rows, holding banners, that read:

Disability

Adisa was a young boy who looked after his family as his father died at a young age. This situation is not unusual for most of the men who live in the Southern province.

Every day, he used to walk for several miles carrying a bulky load of wood, which he chopped. His nearest destination was around five miles away. He never got a respectful profit that was required to cover his family's essentials. His profit was always considered as equivalent to none.

With time he lost half of his weight. He also ended up with a deformed backbone. Adisa kept working day after day till that morning when he couldn't get up, but his younger brother could.

He lost his ability to stand or walk because of the intense pain. Since then he was not seen, like other disabled people, who were usually kept out of sight.

John, at the other end of the world, happily enjoyed fast food, creamy cakes with sugary dribbles that win over any peckish eyes. He didn't take physical activities seriously, including the Physical Education (PE) lessons. The parents were unhappy that the school criticised his weight, which was above the expected parameter for his age.

With time he became so addicted to the extent that it was too late for him to control his will to do anything. His weight steadily doubled. His movement was fast diminished. He started complaining of back and joint pains, sooner than expected.

Both Adisa and John found it extremely hard to find a job they would have enjoyed. They were forced to take the first available opportunity.

On top of all that, it was not unusual to slip into depression. It forced them to live in the shadow, to avoid the much wounding stares from total strangers at pedestrian crossings, for John and across the bumpy roads for Adisa.

Both boys were independently helped to learn digital skills to improve their employability and life prospects.

Later they met through an online chat group. In no time, they became friends. Their friendship extended to their families who shared experiences. They also supported each other despite their geographic remoteness.

Both felt connected, somehow, regardless of their huge differences, not to mention the causes of their disabilities. This tie seemed to be the strongest link. Both continuously felt the pain, witnessing the shock that jumped from the narrow-minded eyes, around them.

Ursula and Lisa were disheartened, as they genuinely felt their despair. Despite the distress, they carried on with the study.

Different Scenarios – Similar Outcomes

This time, they chose to compare the story of Ebony, who lived in the South with Thomas who lived in the North.

Ebony was a well-educated woman who had a high sense of wisdom and reasoning. Thomas had a good education too. However, Ebony was smarter and had a richer experience compared to Thomas.

Ebony accepted the given unwritten rules of her community: got married, had children and said goodbye to her career. She lived a predictable life, depending on her husband's limited income. She never complained.

Thomas, in the North, where many men had the upper hand in the boardroom did very well. He secured a respected status in the business community. Therefore, he had a huge authority as chief executive.

Being an intelligent man, he recognised his authority and deliberately misused it. He never appointed a female colleague for a top job, even though they were fully qualified.

"It should have been a frustrating feeling for women to be treated differently just because of their gender." This was the thought that crossed both Ursula's and Lisa's minds.

"Is it not the mothers who take the most important role in raising up chief executives, who then exclude the women from the boardrooms?" said Ursula.

"They were the same people who do triple working shifts: at home, office, in addition to raising kids but paid only one salary?" Lisa continued. "In market language, it equates to three for the price of one." They laughed.

Both were stunned by the result of the dissimilar scenarios (Ebony versus Thomas), but the similar outcome for women on both sides.

The Trap

Another story was that of Saad, who migrated to the North seeking a freedom. He was forced into a dodgy business that helped launder money and groom young girls and boys online. They also traded in illegal goods and substances.

Jack, from the North, took a gap year to set off towards the South. Whilst he was "googling", he came across Saad who was looking at the same site.

Later, they both discovered they had similar experiences. Jack was also targeted by a specialised, criminal group, who smuggled girls for sex. They also sold illegal substances.

Both businesses targeted vulnerable women and foreigners.

Jack and Saad realised too late, the moment they set foot in such affairs, neither them nor their targets would be able to get out. By then their actions would have ruined their ambitions.

The researchers sympathised with Jack and Saad.

Identity Crisis

The story of Amara is another thing. She was a mixed-race child who lived with her family mid-way between the South and the North. She felt tied up interacting with both sides. She saw herself as better off than one side of the family yet felt pushed away when trying to relate to the other side.

Amara lost herself on the way. Sometimes she felt vulnerable, at others she was transformed into a bully. It was not hard for those around her to spot all the contradictions she tried to hide. They concluded that she was torn between her two identities. She distanced herself from everybody.

Luckily, she was employed by a highly regarded institution far away from both sides of her family. Amara hoped she left the controversial past behind. She failed, even though her colleagues were representing a wide range of culture and identities. She simply felt half/half. She attempted to bury every drop of sadness deep into her subconscious. They became part of her make-up.

Her colleagues accepted her as she was. This gesture gave her confidence.

Amara shined in the new atmosphere, just like a bunch of light. Her apparent happiness was noticed by all, as she felt accepted. The diverse environment helped her to recall her lost self. She was reformed to become both receptive and decisive. Learning to smile was not a challenge for her anymore. She was able to unlock her real self. A pleasant feeling filled her entire body.

Amara strengthened her ability to influence those who listened to her, telling captivating stories. Whenever, she described any view or idea, it just materialised in front of the eyes of her listeners. This was why, when she expressed her thoughts, she had a magical effect on those around her.

One of her intriguing moments was when she let her imagination drift away. She would create, a dream-like tale, believe in it, then retell it.

On her annual leave she made two important journeys to the two places she belonged. Her visit made her stronger. To start with she brushed her teeth before, then after breakfast to satisfy both cultures. (Her family in the North prefer to brush their teeth after breakfast, whilst the family in the South would brush their teeth before breakfast.) Her mouth had the same fresh feel following each brushing.

She wore clothes which belonged to both sides. As expected, they were so different. She ate two types of totally dissimilar food and had the same enjoyment. She visited the zoo and went on a Safari; she felt the same level of excitement. She sensed the same soothing effect, looking at two different waterfalls. She climbed Northern and Southern mountains and experienced the same feeling of anticipation and fear. She visited two schools who taught different but similar alphabets. She heard two different melodies and danced to the rhythm of both with the same level of enjoyment. She felt complete.

Coming back, she shared her magical moments, reading a story to her colleagues, titled, *I am Complete*. The listeners saw, not heard, a one of its kind "visual peace":

"I was carried by mermaids on a silky cradle decorated with rare diamonds that reflected the moon's rays. It took me to a yacht with an open roof space, not to disturb the views. I couldn't believe that I was swaying freely from North to South, surrounded by coloured bubbles rising from the seabed to slowly drifting away.

My laughter resonated a romantic melody that filled the space, witnessing the South calling the North inside me. The amazon forests laid its roots in the beach hugging the melting iceberg.

The view was completed with the drops of rain gently touching the waves in both parallel oceans.

The hypnotised décor enhanced with the innocent laughter of the children singing *Jungle Bells* replacing *Jingle Bells*. To me that was it. It added magic to the panoramic view."

I breathed in, the mixed smell of the Southern pineapple and the aroma of the roses from the North.

Closing her eyes Amara embraced the gentle breeze, which was filled with the smell of the southern and the northern jasmine, which smelled the same. Her lungs expanded to fill the stage, spreading the aroma beyond to be felt by the two researchers.

A loud clap brought her to the stage in front of her audience.

"I am complete now," she made a respectful bow.

Both Ursula and Lisa did the same.

The Unity of the North and the South

Ursula stood up, looked out of the window then returned to her seat. She touched the "page up" key which took her to the start of their research. Lisa did the same.

To their surprise, they found the original row of those who had lost part of their limbs had changed. It had become a multi-coloured one. The song was more or less the same "We are the world ... We are the children who are yet to come ..."

Both concentrated, to understand the phenomena. It was incredible what was there. The original line broke up horizontally into two parts, apparently representing the North and the South. Each one consisted of multi-coloured segments which Ursula assumed represented the common issues. Lisa agreed.

It was also notable that the colour density of the parallel segments was varied. Lisa explained, "By what we observed so far I can guess that the concerns were the same in the North and the South (similar colours), but they represented themselves differently (dissimilar density)."

Before responding, Ursula's eyes captured intensive activities taking place on the screen. An enormous crowd took over the entire screen in both computers, waving in the same way but so different. It did not disturb the harmony of the overall theatrical extravaganza.

"We are the sick and elderly. Who will look after us? Those who usually did are struggling with us overriding their capacity. Their number was diminished following the immigration ban."

A poster from the parallel segment from the South read, "Welcome to the club. Our families used to look after us. The young migrated to improve their lives and that of their families. So, the issue is universal, yet technically varied."

Another placard from the North was pushing forward, "What about the zero contract?" The same coloured, with a different shade, segment, from the South, shouted, "We never had contracts."

"What about the foodbanks that swallowed our towns in the North? ... The opposite side from the South replied, "We call them the Jawami (mosques). People bring food to the mosques. Those in charge distribute the donation to the homeless and the less-abled.

People usually gave dates, aligned with the belief that Muhammad, the Muslim Prophet, had regarded five dates as a source of energy for the day.

Both researchers were so surprised about this revelation. Ursula talked directly to the screen. "That is new. I guess this should have happened decades ago. It surely brings to life the five-a-day advice by doctors to stay healthy?"

The rows of the young voices on both sides used remote controls and mobile phones with different wave lengths to make their voices heard. They tuned in. "We were robbed of our future and opportunities. Our capabilities were wasted by wars, poverty, corruption and pollution to start with. We turned to knives and violent games abandoning education."

In harmony they sang, "We are the world, we are the children ... take your hands off our future," as they moved forward.

A sudden deep silence filled the screen. Then, all rows clinched to each other, mid-way from both poles. The united lines grew wider.

What impressed both researchers, was the fact that the line grew up and down at the same pace erasing the borders between both sides.

Lisa and Ursula took a deep breath and continued mumbling, "Where has all the racism and hatred come from!!!"

They summarised the outcome of their research with one sentence, "It is just a coin with two faces. They are the same but wearing different make-up." Both pressed "share", closed the computers and stared in the dark.

The Unified Tune of

the Jungle and the Desert

A note to the reader: Because life is not black and white, I chose to use a known style, "Symbolism."

I believe this category would set people's imagination free, when they found themselves in an enclosed situation which was difficult to penetrate. Many hurdles could be unlocked using alternative ways.

This story could easily reflect someone's experience if they belonged to a different culture, spoke a different language, had different features, believed in different principles, suffered from psychological issues or just lacked support.

I hope this story helps people to discharge the negative emotions about differences and react positively to what is going on around them.

It is understandable that each person may have their own views and responses. I feel the diversity in interpreting what writers present is healthy. Hope you appreciate that when reading my writings.

You may feel the topic was repetitive, but I am sure you will also notice the diverse responses of different characters. It also depends on the depth of the impact of that issue.

So, set up your own parameters when reading my books.

The Out of Place Gazelle[1]

Rose, was a beautiful gazelle who grew up lonely in a jungle. She didn't have parents or knew of a place where she belonged. A golden cage, in the deep end, was her only life.

She hadn't faced the wolves' spikes, seen the hyenas' cheeky looks all around, neither did she breathe a rotten, soggy air.

Even more, she hadn't witnessed a crocodile attacking a fragile lamb that lost its way and was separated from its mother. With no hesitation, it would engulf that helpless lamb.

That was why she grew up shallow and inward-looking but resisted any attempt from those around to interact with.

Rose struggled to accept the fact that she had to live amongst strangers, as the golden cage always stood between her and the jungle, which was loudly giggling at that sad scenario. At her moments of optimism, she leaned to believe she would eventually adapt somehow. That had never materialised.

Rose stumbled whenever she tried to walk. Her lowest point was when she had to acknowledge her failure to overcome difficult hurdles that pulled her back. A scream inside her boiled, breaking the silence into pieces. Only then she stood still but exhausted.

It was a miracle that she remarkably survived many infuriating moments.

Rose was unable to break away from the past. Her approach to life was tied up, as if to prevent her hovering free.

On a gloomy insignificant evening, the golden cage crumbled to the ground. That night felt dull and spooky because it was a different environment for Rose. For the first time a damp air filled her lungs and a throbbing nauseating sensation overstuffed her stomach.

[1] Gazelle is a small antelope. The name comes from Arabic language. It is used in love poems.

Our friend was unable to adapt to her new situation. She lost interest, begged for help, support or protection. She received no response as she totally cut ties with all. She turned to the sea. As anticipated, it didn't respond opting to ignore the call in a dramatic show. The sea didn't hide its readiness to tender the poor gazelle to its sharks. It just continued its sluggish repetitive headway.

Rose ran as fast as her legs could support her weight, leaving behind that horrible, strange place, as she imagined.

"Goodbye the shiny ebony trees," were Rose's last words.

On the far horizon she spotted sandy hills which reflected the bright sunlight. It seemed as if they were moving backwards, as she progressed towards them.

The gazelle was extremely thirsty, as all the fluid reserves were evaporated from her tiny body. The blood became solid in the arteries and the veins, yet she determined to carry on, walking or crawling forward, desperate to reach her destination.

Rose sobbed without tears as none were left, she screamed without a sound as no energy was there to support the normal function to do so. She coughed without a movement to clear her congested chest.

Rose wiggled to advance forward. She suddenly looked back to discover the rainforest had disappeared. A sense of relief appeared on the horizon.

Rose couldn't believe her eyes when she sighted a palm tree dancing a tango with the boiling air.

"Thank you, gracious God," Rose said. Then ran as fast as an ostrich, the fastest running bird, to land cuddling the boiling water of a lonely oasis. As she touched the moist face, the oasis tears mixed with hers. It seemed as if they had waited too long for this moment to happen. Both experienced a feeling similar to that of craving for a cup of tea on a chilly morning.

The gazelle immersed then pressed her burning face deep into the roasting water. Rose felt deadly calm as she relaxed for the first time in ages. Both started to sing in a delicate, warm voice. They felt they belonged to each other, as they were lonely in the middle of different settings; an oasis seeking a refuge in the heart of a desert together with an occupant of a golden cage, which was born in the heart of a jungle. It was unbelievable how a piece of wilderness found tranquillity and harmony in a desert.

Affection and hope became their shared vision. The desert wiped off the rainforest's sufferings, whilst a slice of it rested on its chest. It unfolded many horrible human tragedies, compared to what the gazelle had seen. It aimed to sooth her anxieties. For how long they had been together was unknown.

On one bright day they heard the jungle footsteps. The oasis was trembling for fear of losing its identity. It headed towards the deep end of the desert. Its friend, the gazelle, was frightened. She wept loudly, "Don't leave me behind. I am part of you. I was rejected once, left feeling a stranger in my own skin. It returned now to destroy me. With you I felt free. I was myself." Silence dominated. Not even an echo came back. It went with "the wind".

That piece of the jungle waited for the oasis to come back, as it sincerely believed the day would come.

It felt as if her companion took part of herself, when it headed towards the endless desert. Similarly, the oasis felt it left a part of itself in the spot where they met. Despite the distance, both felt these parts were stronger than being torn apart.

Rose started a vibrant dance for the first in her life, in response to the strong rhythms of the jungle's drums, which became louder and louder. Then it felt a calming tune coming from where the oasis had gone. Rose was emotionally drained by the mixture of the two feelings, which she experienced at that same moment. She slowly shut her eyes. Her heartbeats swung from side to side with a different speed, in response to both tunes.

A strong heated gale approached from one side, yet a thunder-storm came from the other. Half of her body felt warm whilst the other half felt soaking cold. The narrow part between them felt nothing. Rose was certain she had been cut at the middle into two halves. She switched off any reaction for a brief time.

Suddenly each side shouted loudly at the same time, "You belong to me."

With closed eyes Rose responded, "I can see the bullets, the minefields, genocide, rape and torture were exactly the same in both halves. She shouted louder, "Stop! I belong to both of you. We don't need two splits of a heart. We need only one. Once we were one. It would remain so, no matter what."

"Please listen to your echoes. They were horrible. We need the rainforest to preserve our environment, even land to build the most needed houses, diverse natural resources to lift up ourselves, our communities and our youngest generations from poverty and desperation. We also need all the brain capacities to live not just survive or die prematurely. What we need is to remove the golden cages that sliced our nation into two. We have enough food for all of us if we are responsible and caring. Destruction, war and man-made famine are not in my name ..."

"Not in my name either."

"Add me ..."

"Me too ..."

"Me ..."

"too..."

"Name ..."

"If you agree ... click."

Scary quietness ... then "click ... click ... cli ... ck ... ck ..."

The same song from each half spontaneously oozed. They were naturally fused, creating a sad, yet happy, soft and silky tune. In the background the desert was dancing to the unifying tune and moved towards the jungle:

"Oh ... the Drums of the Jungle, beat

People dance in rain and heat

Dong ... dong ... dong

Beat and beat ... and loud read

Our stories ... walking dead ... horrible deeds ...

Starvation ...

A sopping nation

Blood ... and pain
Oh the drums beat and beat
Tell the story ... childhood
The misery behind palaces' road
Bleeding sores ... guns ... and cold
A shivering baby without a robe
Crying ... Mama ... without a hope
All they need ...
Drops of milk ... blanket ... food ...
Oh the drums beat and beat
A boy was lost
Sleeping rough ... in rain and gust
Dreaming water... cloth and nest
Dreaming change ... for good not best
Oh the drums beat and beat
Without end ... without rest
Tell the stories;
Starvation ... No ... liberation ... who will dare?
Death of nations ... people suffering ... condemnation
Who will care?
Oh the drums ...
Dong ... dong ... dooooooong weak and weary
Died once ...

Then a loud voice came flying, "Don't forget the Winter Blues of different Lenses":
Winter blues ... winter plights
Winter glooms ... winter delights
Evil and good ... wrong and right
You and I have perfect lives ...
Beds are warm
Safe at home
Fish in tanks
Pets around
Tech ... mobiles ...
Gym ... and cinema ...

Games ... and sauna
Designers' genius? ... all are mine ...
Beautiful evening ... relaxed and fine
Fruits ... pancakes ... a glass of wine ...
Lights dimmed... curtains aside
Glancing through my window ... behind
The snow was bright
A magical scene ... a wave of light
Flakes were dancing ...
The wind enchanting ...
Winter glooms? ... Also ... divine
Across that road ... a homeless man ... was curling aside
Frightened ... lonely ...
Feeling abundant ... to winter blues ... that always bite ...
A girl was waiting ...
The wind was raging ...
The rain and thunder ...
The road was empty ...
The home was rusty ...
The bed was cold ...
The room was dusty
Returning home? ... the soul was empty ...
Winter blues? ...
Winter blights?
Winter glooms? ... that is right ...
A boat was packed and rushed at night
Swinging left ... swinging right
Scared of bombs ... escaping fight
"The shore," they said ... "will be ... alright"
The boat had left ... and souls had died
The day was cold, snowed at night
Few were safe ... dreaming peace ... sleep not fight
Winter glooms? ...
Winter plights?
Winter blues ... remain inside ... A daily plea ...

The homes were lost ... no hopes ... no rights
Winter glooms ...
Winter bright ...
Winter truth ...
Winter plights ...
Winter blues ... different frights

Hamiha Haramiha

When the Protector is the Thief

This is a short-lived reflection due to the many restrictions. It is an unfinished story, as the battle for power engulfs all sides. The victim is dying anyway, maybe from the shock of the reality.

It is about Todd and Emma.

Todd occupied a top position in an establishment that was supposed to support people who were less fortunate than others.

Despite the honourable goal of the rulers of the city, Todd regularly betrayed those in his custody. He was a very hard man whose heart was wrinkled by being a two-faced person. For those who were dependent on him, he was regarded as the gatekeeper. Only a few saw the truth about him, a power follower and grabber at any cost.

His look was scary, to the extent that it caused discomfort for people around him. This was not because of his natural features. It was due to the burden which he voluntarily chose to carry over his shoulders. His actions amused, any powerful devil, the least.

Whenever things happened in real life to real people, disasters strike. Some people have no choice, but to accept the hard truth, that these things usually happen to individuals like them.

This situation reminded us of the feeling, when an illusion was accepted as a reality.

A bridge collapsed with no one claiming responsibility. A building engulfed in a fire with a devastating impact on many communities. All that happened because, corrupt and dishonest heads of establishments, like Todd, crossed over the safety barriers, giving up on their own people. Then they happily washed their hands and continued, as before.

It was hard to believe when, Todd, the next day led a huge rally in the name of the same people. He had sold them cheaply, seeking promotion to a higher position.

He worked hand in hand with Emma, who was very offensive when interacting with people. Like Todd, she knew how to change her colour just like the chameleon to suit any eventuality. She studied criminology and learned how to find her way in and out of any sticky situation.

People wondered how they could wipe the truth from within their own souls, like wiping out a document from a computer, despite the back-up arrangements.

They look you in the eye and say, "We can't find a trace of your *life experience.*" It was kept in the safest secure self-storage unit! You would think, "As if it could fade away, despite the strong security arrangements." The missing link was that they had access to it.

That is why those who sought sanctuary from people like Todd and Emma, saw them as judge and defendant at the same time. It was a horrible reality.

So, victims felt it is right to call this piece *Hamiha Haramiha*, as a popular saying in many places they belonged to.

A message the Reader: There was no traditional start and end to this piece as the state of affairs is repetitive everywhere. In the current era there are no prospects of addressing this issue.

Maybe in the coming thirty years someone will be brave enough to come forward. Then the Court may open the cases with no hope of resolution and the same circle would start again.